Francis Adams

Songs of the Army of the Night

.

Francis Adams

Songs of the Army of the Night

ISBN/EAN: 9783744767545

Printed in Europe, USA, Canada, Australia, Japan

Cover: Foto ©Andreas Hilbeck / pixelio.de

More available books at **www.hansebooks.com**

'IT WAS THE PRINCESS ONDINE.'—*Page* 62.

HARRY'S BIG BOOTS.

A Fairy Tale.

WITH ILLUSTRATIONS BY THE AUTHOR.

London:

SAMUEL TINSLEY, PUBLISHER,

10, SOUTHAMPTON STREET, STRAND.

HARRY'S BIG BOOTS.

A Fairy Tale, for "Smalle Folke."

By S. E. GAY.

WITH ILLUSTRATIONS BY THE AUTHOR,
DRAWN ON WOOD BY PERCIVAL SKELTON.

Brief bee-like flights in search of pleasure bent,
"From blossoms wild, of fancies innocent."

LONDON :

SAMUEL TINSLEY, 10, SOUTHAMPTON ST., STRAND.

1874.

LONDON: PRINTED BY
EDWARD J. FRANCIS, TOOK'S COURT,
CHANCERY LANE, E.C.

PREFACE.

———◆———

THERE needs no "Author's apology" for
aught written for the young. The mind of
childhood contains no criticism; it enjoys:
the heart of childhood possesses no cynicism;
it believes. It would seem thus a wasteful
weariness to give a recondite meaning to
what will be received with a single-hearted
simplicity, were it not that a parable may
ever be either a tale or a sermon, losing
nothing of the sweetness of the first for the
earnestness of the latter.

I am indebted to accounts of that most
wondrous process of Deep-Sea Dredging for
the fancied freaks of a "Miss Willowy-
Billowy" and a "Miss Wavy-Cavey";—to
any floating fragment of modern science,
for the desert land of Rory-Tory Island

with its weird inhabitant;—to a note or two
of the minor key in the chords of life, for
the brief suggestion of Shadow-land.

Wearied in spirit, these little fairy-flights
of mingled fact and fancy have been woven
together by my desultory pen as a recrea-
tion and a solace from hour to hour. My
only wish in rendering them up to the
sterner custody of print, is to make some
little child laugh.

S. E. G.

October, 1873.

CONTENTS.

LIST OF ILLUSTRATIONS.

HARRY'S BIG BOOTS.

CHAPTER I.

HOW HE FOUND THEM.

It was a summer afternoon. The spot was
charming,—a little glade by a brook-side,
carpeted with grass, softer than green velvet,
as soft as only the very softest moss can be,
decked gaily, too, with blue forget-me-nots
and yellow buttercups, and overhung by
the broad sprays of beech-branches, which
stretched out their long arms from the stately
trees which grew around. It was almost
like a bower, but a great deal prettier than
any artificial bower could be, because it
allowed the sunshine to come streaming
through in bright gleams, till it fell on the

B

brown water of the brook, and sent all the little
trout in it to sleep. They had been very
much frightened a moment or two before, for
Harry had brought his fishing-rod,—*he* well
knew all the nicest spots in the wood,—and
had nearly succeeded in catching the biggest
of them all. No wonder. He was such a
silly fish, and felt so sure that nice tempting
bait was intended especially to please him;
it looked *so* delicious, just like a piece of
toffy with almonds in it, or a piece of plum-
cake, would have been to Harry; and as for
the "hook" that he had heard such a lot of
old tales about, why he didn't believe a word
of it, or at any rate he shouldn't believe it
till he saw it. So he swam straight off to
the feast, and was just going to commence
operations when it gave a great jerk, and at
the same time all the other little fishes cried
out "Oh, don't!" in such an appealing and
pathetic style that it gave him a fright, and
he darted off under the roots of the green
grass, and hid for a long while, throbbing all
over and fanning himself with one fin to
try to recover himself. The fact was, at that

very moment Eliza, the nurse, had arrived
on the scene with Harry's little dot of a
sister, Lily; and as they came crashing
through the boughs quite suddenly,—for you
could not see anybody in this snug little spot
till they came right into it,—it had startled
Harry, and he moved his rod just as the
foolish big trout was going to nibble.

"There!" said Harry, "you've made me
lose my trout, and now it's of no use fishing any
more, so I shall go to sleep," saying which,
he threw down his rod and line and stretched
himself out at full length on the mossy bank,
with his hat over his eyes, and pretended he
was quite lost to the world around him. I say
pretended, as Harry, like many other young
folks, was fond of "making-believe" to do
things—why, I don't know—and he fancied
there was some kind of merit attached to the
fact that he, being supposed asleep, should
take no notice whatever of the conversation
of Eliza and his little sister. It was rather
hard work, however. Lily, having gathered
as many flowers as her little hands could hold,
stole over to brother Harry, to see if he *would*

" wake-up " and help to amuse her. She lifted up his hat and peeped underneath; and it was as much as Harry could do to keep grave, but he would not have laughed for the world; and then she stuck buttercups into all the button-holes of his coat and waist-coat, till he looked like a May Queen gone mad. He longed to say " Don't, Lily," only it would have been undignified ; but he began to find the flies and gnats worse " teasers " still; they hummed incessantly right over his very nose, and now and then one would settle on it. and tickle dreadfully. It was all poor Harry could do to endure it; but then the glory of remaining like a wax image ! Like some other people, he liked to imagine he was doing a duty when in reality he was only making himself uncomfortable. If it *had* been a duty, I am not at all so sure Master Harry would have been quite so brave about it. At last, when he was beginning to wonder how long he should have to " keep on," whiz ! came a great *bumble-bee* right into his ear, which it evidently mistook for a flower, as it kept buzzing and whizzing

there, and trying to get inside, as if it was
a matter of life and death for it. Up sprang
Harry, and shook himself tremendously,
screaming out "Oh!" and "Bother!" as if
he were very much frightened, but in reality
rather glad to be relieved from his self-im-
posed "duties," and quite ready to enjoy a
new lease of life and fishing. Down fell all
his fringes of buttercups, away darted all the
little trout, and Lily danced a mad little
dance of joy round him, which, as she was
not particularly careful where she was going,
or what was the condition of her outer gar-
ments, ended in her tumbling down *very* near
the brook, and *quite* losing her loosely-tied
hat, which fell into it. The hat seemed
determined, now it had " gone and been and
done it," to enjoy itself as well as it could
under the circumstances, and prepared in
consequence for a nice jaunt ever so far
down the brook; *only,* just as it was beginning to swim, it didn't see where it was
going, and the brook spitefully sent it up
against a large stone, and kept it there.
" *Squish!*" was all it said, and then it dole-

fully filled half full of water, and looked as
if it was going to sink down and faint away
on the spot. It began then to remember its
dear little mistress, and felt rather sorry it
had been in such a hurry to leave her and
see life. Though she *did* bang it about a
little, and hold it dangling by the strings,
and had certainly once or twice sat upon it
by mistake, still it knew she meant kindly
and hadn't seriously intended ever to do it
an injury. These were sad thoughts. As for
Lily, her two little round blue eyes sparkled
with a little diamond tear, one in each eye;
and they were preparing to keep company
down her rosy cheeks when a loud "hurrah!"
from Harry frightened them back again into
their two little houses, and sent a thrill of
hope right through every fibre of the drowning
hat. The fact was, Master Harry was very
busy taking off his shoes and stockings as
fast as ever he could, thinking it tremendous
fun to have a paddle—a regular "good time"·
in the brook. Old Eliza reminded "Master
Harry" that it was "only three months
since he had had the measles." "I wouldn't

go in that there brook," added she, " if you'd *pay* me—full of horrid live things which may bite you, not to say but you'll stick in the mud, and then *I* shan't pull you out." Eliza always said that. According to her, nobody had ever been helped if she had once "told them so" in her life; it was very funny, too, but quite true, that she always helped more people out of their scrapes than anybody else. However, Harry managed to remember that somebody had said sometime that cold water was the best thing in the world when you were recovering from the measles; and as for the "things" in the brook, they were much more likely to be afraid of him than he should be of them, and so forth. Accordingly he gave a great jump, and went—splash !—into the very middle, and waded till he came to the spot where the hat was, and caught fast hold of it. "Oh, how glad I am !" exclaimed the hat to itself; " I was just fainting away ! In fact, I should have died half a minute later." All this, however, sounded only just like "*screeze—squilch,*" as Harry took it up and squeezed the water out of it. Then

he waded back again opposite Lily, and threw
it at her.   "O I'm a bird, I'm flying!"
cried the vain old hat, and then it alighted
helplessly at her feet, where, let us hope, it
settled down in a more becoming spirit.
Poor Eliza now urged Master Harry to come
ashore, but he wouldn't : it was so delightful
being in the water and doing what you liked
in it, which you couldn't on dry land; and,
besides, he could now, perhaps, catch the
big trout with his net, and that would be a
great advantage.   The trout, however, were
far too dismayed even to think of the most
enticing supper that could be placed before a
fish.   At the first sight of Harry's pink legs,
they had all huddled away ever so far up the
brook, screaming, "Oh, how dreadful!" and
"Do let us hide!" till they found a nice
quiet pool to rest in.   The big trout felt particularly put out of countenance, and as soon
as he found himself safely surrounded by his
companions gave them a piece of his mind.

"I always thought," said he, "that the
two-legged creatures dwelt on land.   Now
that they have taken to the water, it will be

quite dangerous to go out. What are the times coming to?"

Meanwhile, Harry, who found his trout had fled, and felt the water rather too cold to be pleasant, had landed near a large stone, bleached white with many a winter's flood and summer's ripple, and here and there patched with beautiful little tufts of moss, with the idea of walking back on the bank till he rejoined his nurse, Eliza, and his little sister. He had not pushed his way through the long grass and overhanging branches very far before he came upon an old-fashioned pair of high boots, much the worse for wear, but still wearable, and which seemed of all others the very thing for wading. "A fairy must have put them there," cried he. "Now I shall be able to wade whenever I like." Whereupon he seated himself on the bank and took up one to look at. Directly he touched it, it gave a little hop. "How funny!" thought Harry; but he did not feel in the least alarmed. Then the other gave a little hop, too; and then with one voice they both began to speak. "We are the

celebrated Seven-league Boots," they cried
both in a breath; "and if you put us on, we
will take you ever so far—right round the
world and back again, and show you all
kinds of strange and curious things which
you would never think of."

"All right," said Harry, "there's nothing
I should like better. I shall have jolly long
holidays now, and I think it will be awful
fun, only"—here he felt a little bit low-
spirited—"I think I should like to say
good-bye first to Lily and Mamma and Eliza.
They would wonder where I was."

"We can do this on our way," replied the
Boots, in a most condescending manner;
"only put us on, as it's high time we were
on our travels, and we have been idling
a long while here by this stone. We can go
nowhere without legs, though you might
think we were quite independent, and legs
could go nowhere without us. It's rather a
nuisance," added the right Boot reflectively,
"but it is the natural consequence of a
foolish state of things. It will be all right
when we—"

"When what? Are worn out?" asked Harry, curiously.

"When," said the Boots, yawning tremendously, "we get to the other end of everywhere." Upon this they yawned more and more till they looked as if they were going to swallow up poor Harry, who, however, made the best of it, and, showing a firm front, gave each of them a little kick, which they took advantage of to fasten firmly on to his legs. They were rather big, certainly, in the upper part, but they contracted below till they fitted his feet to a nicety; and *what* an advantage it was to have not only a pair of "grown-up" big Boots, but Boots that were so sagacious and contriving that they knew how to go round the world! Never had Harry felt so elated before. The fishing-rod, the big trout, and the pretty glade in the wood were all alike forgotten.

CHAPTER II.

OUT INTO THE GREAT WORLD.

"Which is the way?" asked the Boots. "To the left," answered Harry, and they immediately gave a great skip, which took him straight to his Mamma and Lily, who had been taken home by Eliza, and had had her hat well dried by the fire. Never before had Harry gone such a long way with so little trouble; it was delightful. He had only to say he wanted to go somewhere, and hop! off went the Boots like twenty prize race-horses knocked into one, which would make something *almost* as strong as a steam-engine. His Mamma didn't seem in the least surprised. She was sitting by the drawing-room window working, and when she saw Harry and he told her he was going

round the world, she only said, " Mind
you're back in time for tea," in the most
natural manner possible, and went on sewing.
Harry then told the Boots to take him "into
the world," and felt very grand as he said
so. He had very vague notions as to what
it was; it came first in his atlas he knew,
and meant there Europe, Asia, Africa, and
America; but he had heard the clergyman
in church say that we were not to think
about " the world," which seemed contra-
dictory, as he had most decidedly to choose
between thinking about it or getting a
thrashing from Mr. Coachwell, his school-
master; and, finally, his Mamma had often
told him that when he grew up he would
have to go into the world, and he must try
to be a wise, good man, as there were a
great many " snares " in it for foolish people.
Harry thought that snares meant something
like bird-traps, put to *catch* you, so that
altogether, what with the might-be thrash-
ings and large bird-traps, the world seemed
but a sorry sort of place, and his ideas on
the subject were very confused, poor fellow.

Still, having heard about it, he naturally felt a little curious, and then the Boots had indicated to him there were "a great many things to be seen, and, besides, if he didn't see the world, where *was* he to go and what *was* he to see?"

The Boots, however, stood quite still, much to his discomfiture, and never gave the least little bit of a tiny hop in any direction.

" Why don't you go?" asked Harry, in dismay, and thinking they had taken him in after all, and couldn't go nearly so far as they made out.

" Because you 're *in* it," replied the Boots. Harry felt fairly puzzled. Was he in the map, after all?—and where were the snares? he didn't see any,—and ought he to think about where he was? O dear, how puzzling it was! "I don't understand you," he exclaimed, in very disappointed tones; "please explain."

" Why, all that you see is the world—all around you," cried the Boots, laughing; and giving one a great fling to the left, and the other a great fling to the right. "What we promised was to show you some queer things in different parts of it that you 've never seen before."

"Well, then, take me at once," exclaimed Harry; "I am longing to see something wonderful, and you know I have to be back in time for tea."

Hop! whiz! whirr!—away flew the Boots, without another word. Oh, how fast they went—past towns and villages, and fields full of cows and sheep—it was just like being in a railway train, only ever so much nicer, as, if there was anything interesting to see, Harry had only to tell the Boots, and stop to see it. He, however, did not say anything till after the hop seemed to have lasted a long while, and carried them a great way, and then he inquired of the Boots where they were going to in particular.

"To Rory-Tory Island," said the Boots; "we shall soon get there. It's the funniest place in the world." And presently, in truth, they left the land altogether, and scudded at a great rate through the air, and high over

the sea, which looked so deliciously blue that
Harry was tempted to stop and propose they
should take a dip in it, as he had often heard
it was full of wonderful things; but the Boots
replied that they would go there afterwards,
and that they had been there once before,
and instead of being quite cold and pitch-
black, a long way down it was most pleasant;
and as for the society, it was charming.
Harry's attention was now arrested by the
sight of a dull, dim, flat, sandy-looking patch
beginning to spread out like a map towards
the horizon; and as they came nearer, he
saw it was a large low island, without so
much as a bush or a tree on it, and nothing
in the world that was in the least pretty to
be seen.   He felt almost indignant with the
Boots for bringing him such a long way to
see nothing, and he *did* say to them that it
seemed very uninteresting; to which the
Boots replied, that this was the well-known
Rory-Tory Island, and that it contained a
very wonderful sight, as he would see if he
had only patience to walk quietly—as they
wanted a rest—up the beach to the place

where it was to be found. Accordingly they
landed, and Harry, guided by the Boots,
who were panting a good deal, and creaked
dreadfully, wound his way over a long reach
of round pebbles, all exactly alike, up to
some sand-hills, which were very small and
all of precisely the same size and pattern,
too. He went up and down, and up and
down, a great many times, till he began to
feel quite tired (for the Boots could only
help him a little till they had quite recovered
from their fatigue), and wondered when he
should get to the end of them. At last, just
as he was beginning to feel rather cross again,
they came to a large flat space, all sand, in
the midst of which was built a small stone
pyramid, on the top of which was seated a
very queer-looking old man. It *was* an odd
sight, and so Harry thought. As they came up
to him he seemed to recognize the Boots, and
said, "How d'ye do" to them very affably, but
he took no notice of Harry. The Boots then
approached close enough for Harry to have
a good view of him, and commenced a conversation. "How do you feel?" they asked.

"Much the same," replied the queer-looking old man, "only rather drier than usual. But the view is lovely, and that keeps my spirits up."

Harry didn't agree with this at all, but he didn't like to question it, especially as it would, perhaps, have the effect of taking away the only solace that the poor old man seemed to have, so he asked the Boots in a whisper who he was, and if he always sat on the pyramid. "Why, he's the great Evolution-man," they replied, also in a whisper; and then correcting themselves, explained—"The man who has grown out of the pyramid. He's called Primitive Prim in consequence. Look here"; and with that they marched round to the other side of the pyramid, and Harry saw a little hole, with a little iron spade hung up on a hook close by, and a pair of spectacles. "He found out the story in the hole, so he says. A lot of little things inside the hole came out and chattered in their language that they remembered him when he was just like them—poor little creeping periwinkles; but

I think it was their vanity, don't you? But you ask him all about it. He'll be sure to tell you, as he is very proud of the discovery, strange to say, and is fond of talking about it."

Harry couldn't imagine how anybody could be proud of having been a periwinkle, though a periwinkle might like to think it could grow into a man, but he plucked up courage to face the old fellow, and ask him a few things.

Primitive Prim shook his ancient grey beard and rubbed his bald head, and looked at him very solemnly, saying, "Take care what you say to me; I'm a very venerable being. I've been here for ages, and have come up gradually out of the pyramid, which is very clever of me."

"How do you know you did?" asked Harry; "and what makes you so fond of being here?"

"The periwinkles," replied Primitive Prim, "who have been extremely kind, or I shouldn't be as wise as I am now, informed me that they had bones inside them, and a pair of eyes for seeing with; and as I have too, it is quite clear I must have been a periwinkle myself once; only I fortunately crawled outside, and the moon shone on me, so that I grew bigger and bigger, till I became the important creature you see before you."

"I didn't think moonshine was good for anything," said the Boots, in a whisper; "but don't you tell him so."

"I don't remember all this," said the old fellow, yawning, "but the winkles do, and they often remind me of our old play-days together. They say I was cross at first when I lost my shell; and then, when I put on my spectacles, I saw their eyes staring at me, so that as I had eyes too, and felt my bones ache,—which at my time of life have become much modified, that is, changed, you know, by sitting on the pyramid and kicking my heels about,—I saw no reason to doubt their story. I *must* have come from *somewhere.*"

"Dear me!" cried Harry; "well this *is* a queer thing; and how did the little periwinkles got there? From the sea, I suppose; they generally stick fast where they find stones."

"O, no; not at all," replied Primitive Prim; "some of the stones of the pyramid got jumbled together somehow, and made a powder which grew into winkles of its own accord."

"How knowing!" exclaimed Harry; "why, now I think of it, it seems the most likely thing in the world. Of course! Only, how did the pyramid come here to begin with, and what's the meaning of it? It *looks* as if it meant something, and had been done by somebody."

"I have examined that too with my spectacles," replied Primitive Prim, "and I think it's made of fog, baked hard. I expect the sun did it."

"Why," said Harry, "then *you* must be made of fog, after all!"

Primitive Prim wagged his head very ferociously at this, and replied, "I am a very venerable old man, and know a great deal about the pyramid. You're rather rude."

"So it seems," said saucy Harry; "but you admit you *are* fog, and of course your notions must be foggy!"

"This is unseemly," rejoined Primitive Prim; "if I were not so stiff in the joints I should get off my pyramid and thrash you with my spectacles." Harry thought that it would be bad for the spectacles, but he didn't say so, and he ventured to inquire, in a tone more befitting the venerable Prim's solemn demeanour, "how long he meant to stay there?" and "what his prospects were generally?"

"I can't say how long I may sit here," he replied, rather more pleasantly; "but I *may* gradually turn back into a large periwinkle again; and if I am able to curl round, I shall make a very respectable fossil."

"Oh!" said Harry; "and then I suppose you'll go back into the powder, and after that into the fog."

"Just so," replied Primitive Prim, in an animated manner. "Ah! it's a grand idea, turning from a winkle to a primitive old person like me, and from a primitive old

party back again to a winkle, with a prospect
of being a curled-up fossil into the bargain !
I'm going to take a nap over the idea." So
saying, he suddenly gave a sort of neat
wriggle, till nothing was to be seen of him
but his venerable bald pate, and his two
venerable feet, having skilfully adapted himself to a large hole in the pyramid much to
his intense satisfaction. Just as he was muf-
fling himself up for his doze, he squeaked out
—" If you pass by this way again, come and
see me as a fossil ! I *shall* be a sight then!"

Harry and the Boots thought so too, and
with one joyful skip of relief, and a great
" whiz," they fled apace from Rory-Tory
Island !

CHAPTER III.

OVER THE BLUE SEA.

AWAY they flew! far over the desert sand-
hills and the pebbly beach, far over the blue
salt waves and up into the soft blue sky, till
Primitive Prim's melancholy island became
as a dim purple cloud on the verge of the
horizon, set about everywhere by the voiceful
borders of the far-spreading sea.

It seemed half sad to Harry to leave the
poor old man thus desolate in his tiny desert
world, where never a bird came with glad
note and joyous wing to sing its song to him,
and never a flower raised its rosy crest to
gladden his feeble eyes. He could not help
giving utterance to his thoughts as they flew
along, and asked the Boots with wonder
why he seemed so contented with his lot,

THEY FLEW OVER THE ELUE SEA.' —*Page 24.*

and how it was the island was so bleak and ugly and barren.

"Don't pity him," replied the Boots; "he does not see things as you do; nobody who was so fond of an ugly old pyramid, and believed they belonged to it so completely, ever could. If he had ever such a quantity of beautiful flowers and birds and trees and pleasant sights and sounds, it would make no difference to him. He would only think they were like himself, pieces of the pyramid that had happened to grow somewhere else, and he would not care for them as people do who see things as they are, which is the best way to see them if they are to make us happy. He *would* go and live in that dreary island all alone, and he likes it better than anything else; so the best way is not to interfere with him, and to let him find out how dull it is after he has been there a good long while."

Away they flew!—they had got a long way above the sea now, and it seemed to Harry as if they were going to pay a visit to the moon; so at last he said, "Do you know, I

think we are going to the moon, and it will
be very much out of our way, and I 'm afraid
mamma will be angry."

" The *moon*; oh, dear, no," cried the Boots;
" why, it 's ever so many hundred miles off
yet, perhaps more. We could not go there
without a portmanteau full of our best clothes,
as we should have to make a long visit."

" I thought," said Harry, " you never
went more than seven leagues at a time.
How is it you take such *very* big long hops
now? I have read about the Seven-league
Boots, and they couldn't go half so far as
you do."

" We are *descended* from the original
Seven-league Boots," replied the Boots, with
natural pride, " and keep up the name, but
we have much improved on our great-grand-
fathers, as our family have always adapted
themselves to the times, which required us to
go a *great* deal quicker than they did. If
they hadn't, I expect by this time we should
have died out altogether in an old lumber-
room."

" Well," said Harry, who grew more and

more surprised at the newly displayed powers
of the Boots, " suppose we don't fly quite so
high. I seem to be getting quite giddy and
out of breath, and besides, I like to look at
the sea and the big waves, and watch the
great sea-gulls dipping their bills and ducking
into the water."

" All right," rejoined the amiable Boots,
and down they came, nearer and nearer to
the blue sea, over which they were hastening,
till at last Harry almost thought they should
tumble into it. As they came closer, he beheld a little dark speck floating on the water
in the distance, which soon appeared to be a
dear little ship, with a string tied to it, which
went down into the water.

" Oh, how I should like to take it home
and sail it on the pond!" cried Harry; "do,
pray, let us stop and have a look at it!"
Upon this the Boots settled quite quietly
down on the top of a big wave which was
rolling straight towards it, so that they had
a good rest, and Harry a capital view of all
that was going on. It turned out to be bigger
than it looked, and wasn't exactly a toy-ship

after all, for there were a good many people
on board, who seemed to be very busy.   As
Harry came closer, he was able to see what
they were doing.   He saw several charming
old gentlemen poking at a mass of mud which
lay on the deck, and every now and then they
said, " Oh, what a duck!   What a beauty!
How glad we are to see you!   Do come in
and take off your things!" and carefully
fished out something from the midst of the
pile, which they placed on a large washstand.   Harry thought from this they must
be some valuable kind of pearls, and he was
very much astonished when he came nearer
still to find the washstand quite full of little
brown dabs of sponges and a small sea-urchin
or two.   They were very neatly ranged all
in a row.   As soon as the old gentlemen had
found all they could, they flew to the washstand, and commenced scrubbing these poor
little things with some tooth-brushes, in four
or five large basins of water (once or twice
the sea-urchins squeaked out, as it was not
the sort of thing they had been accustomed
to, and they were rather frightened, but the

old gentlemen said " Hush!" in such a pleasant, kind manner, and promised them so
sweetly that they should be labelled and go
to the British Museum as soon as ever it
could be managed, that they felt quite re-
assured); and after they had been scrubbed
till they shone, their kind hosts provided
several little houses full of water for them
to live in, and tucked them up in bed, and
wished them good-night. On the outside of
the houses, which were made of transparent
glass, was written " Nice Pickling Inside."
So I suppose the sponges and all the little
sea-urchins were pickled.

" Why do they do this ?" asked Harry ;
" and what is it for ?"

" Well," said the Boots, " they want to
know who lives at the bottom of the sea
now, as they think the inhabitants may be,
after all, nice respectable little people ; so
they send down a large bag, with an invitation to the best sea-urchins and their
families to pay a visit to their ship for
change of scene and air, and you see these
are among the number who have accepted."

"But suppose," said Harry, "the *very* nicest shouldn't come; and they would never know, it's such a long way off. Don't you think if you wanted to see the people who live in the sea, the best way would be to go there?"

"Certainly," replied Boots; "but then you see there are different names for things. The old gentlemen aren't fitted to take such long journeys, and giving an invitation to the sea-urchins they call Science; but if the sea-urchins were to invite *them*, and *they* were to go, they would call that Drowning, and the two things are not exactly alike."

"So this is Science," said Harry, sighing. "I think it must be very dull for the sea-urchins who accept, always being washed and then put to bed. Do they never do anything else?"

"No; never," replied the Boots.

"Then," said Harry, "let *us* do something new, and pay a visit to them. You promised to show me all the wonderful things there are ever so far down, right at the bottom of the deep sea."

"Very well," said the Boots; "but first I must make inquiries of the Sea-gull who is swimming towards us, and ask whether the water is pretty comfortable to-day; sometimes it isn't at all. Hi! Mr. Sea-gull, how is it going with *you* now? Has any news come up lately from your part of the world?"

The Sea-gull swam up quite slowly, pursed up his bill, and looked in the air, first to the right and then to the left. "H'm!" said he, "I think you might venture, if you're thinking of diving. Might be worse, you know. Great nuisance this teasing little vessel, isn't it? It's frightened away—upon my word, I don't exaggerate in the least — no less than eleven as good fat fish as you'd wish to eat for your Sunday dinner, and just as they were right under my very nose. I'm going to take a weed now, to console myself; good-bye." So saying, he picked up a piece of floating sea-weed, stuck it on one side in his pert little bill, and pretending to puff a great deal, paddled off, smoking, as he called it, at a great rate.

"What a conceited little fellow," cried Harry, immensely amused. But he had hardly finished the speech before the Gull, who never could resist the temptation of hearing his own tongue wag, turned sharply round, and exclaimed, " They, over the way there," pointing with his left wing to the vessel, " ought to be stopped—put down, you know. You've no idea what mischief they're doing. Government ought to take it up. Why, an old porpoise, a great friend of mine, came to me this morning—this I assure you is a *fact*—half fainting with fright and as white as a sheet, and said she to me, ' Well, of *all* the things, what do you think has happened now? I was taking my bath as usual this morning, and splashing about the water a great deal; which, I suppose, with my deafness, too, prevented me from hearing the horrid thing; when, just as I turned round, what should I hear—I was obliged to hear *then*— but the most fearful shriek, and *such* a puffing and blowing, from a horrid machine with black smoke coming out of its mouth. And

before I could get away, I saw it put down
a dreadful claw, and heard it cry out,
"Let's catch the old party." Oh, how
I rushed away; and when I got quite out
of sight of the creature, I was obliged to
take brandy-and-water,—which, fortunately,
I always keep in my pocket,—to help me
to recover myself.' And she was palpi-
tating even *then*," said the Gull, shaking
his head in a most solemn manner. "I'm
a bird of the world, and I know enough
to tell me this sort of thing should be put
down. On the first opportunity I mean
to bring it before the Whales. A lash or
two of *their* tails, and yonder little boat—
I call it—would soon be upset. Have a
weed? No?—then, good-bye, again." Saying which, he shook his left wing indignantly
in the direction of the poor little ship,
which was sailing peacefully on its way,
and from whose terror-striking "mouth,"
as the porpoise described it, stole a little
steaming cloud of white vapour, on which
the rays of the setting sun fell, till it looked
like a golden streamer bearing some mes-

D

sage of holiday fun—some glad message to poor overworked folk, who find such happy days too few and far between. Such as you may see, indeed, at the mastheads of all the ships on the Queen's birthday—a pretty sight, in sooth!

And as for the sea-urchins, they had certainly come a long way, and let us hope they were enjoying their visits in their new little houses in proportion to the expense and pains of their journey.

CHAPTER IV.

DOWN IN THE DEPTHS OF IT.

"Now then," said the Boots, manfully, "you must go right head over heels and take a dive. We'll stand on the tip-top of the highest wave you can see, and then you must jump straight off into the little valley alongside."

So Harry *did* stand as he was directed, the Boots helping him to balance nicely, and not without some little feeling of wonder—we won't say fright, for what was there to be afraid of in going to pay a visit to the people who lived·in the beautiful caves down at the bottom of the blue sea, and who would be sure to be glad to see him, and hear the latest news from the upper world?—he gave a great jump and a plunge, and down they

went, just like an express train, whirling away
further and further down into the beautiful
cool waters. It was some time before Harry
got accustomed to the bubbling noise in his
ears, and the rushing, " swishing " sound
they made in going at their usual terrific
pace; but when he did, and had time to look
around him, he found it vastly more pleasant
than he could have imagined.

In the first place, instead of being dark
and disagreeable, the sea was of the most
lovely green-blue colour, but so transparent
that it looked like a piece of stained-glass
window when the sun shines through it; and
instead of being darker, it grew lighter and
brighter, and more beautiful, as they went
down. Harry was surprised at this, and
asked the Boots how it was there seemed so
much sunshine in the sea; and they replied
that he would see presently when they came
near the Sun-fish. And true enough, they
hadn't gone very much further down before
the most dazzling golden light shone all
around them; and looking towards the west,
Harry saw a most brilliant creature, shaped

something like a fish, floating in the water, which had a body sparkling all over in shades of gold and blue and green, and two eyes like diamonds. Never had he seen such a wonderful sight before ; and in fact it's impossible to describe it, as the colours were more like what the chandelier makes on the wall on a sunny afternoon than anything else. Although it was a great way off, it seemed very large ; and Harry inquired, rather anxiously, of the Boots if there was any chance of its seeing them, and perhaps gobbling them up, as it was of such a size that it seemed as if it would often want a good meal. But the Boots replied that the Sun-fish always remained in the same spot, which was a great advantage to the inhabitants of the deep sea, as they had constant light, and could go to bed or stay up just as they chose, which was very convenient. The Boots also added that the Sun-fish was well known for his amiability, as Harry might see for himself in the affable countenance he possessed, and that he never ate up even the tiniest fish, but fed entirely on the choicest

sea-weeds, which were brought to him every
day in large baskets by three good-natured
Whales, who were fond of him, and considered he was an institution which ought to
be supported.

And now Harry also noticed after they
left the neighbourhood of the Sun-fish, and
went still further down, that the sea became
warmer and pleasanter each moment. It was
most delicious, and tasted or felt, in some
indescribable way, just like the sweetest roses
and lilies smell; such charming "scents!"
—where could they all come from? The
Boots said that they were now getting very
near Deep-Sea Town, and that it was
caused by emanations from the beautiful
groves which were planted all round it.
And before Harry had time to wander about
it any more,—lo and behold!—down they
came into the midst of a wonderful region
of arched rocks and waving branches, and
beheld a number of people moving in and
out of them in all directions, and trying to
get out of their way. They landed in what
was evidently the principal street, nearly

tumbling over a piece of cord, which looked
big enough to be the chief clothes-line of the
place; and ere Harry had recovered his surprise at all the new things around him, he
found himself close by a group of mermaid
young ladies, who were raising their voices
to such a pitch and scolding one another so
that they hadn't so much as seen him and
the Boots flying down to them. They were
evidently having a great altercation about
something, so Harry thought it would be the
best plan to stand still and listen, and the
Boots quite agreed. The two who were
making the most noise and raised their
voices highest were two handsome young
mermaids, one of which was seated in state
upon something which looked like a large
leather bag, with a fringe of tassels spread
out behind, but which, it appeared, was a
new carriage she had lately set up, and of
which she was very proud, as it was considered the most stylish thing in Deep-Sea
Town. Three cuttle-fish held fast to the
fringes behind, and were evidently her black
footmen, and a fat sea-urchin, with a fresh,

new livery on, sat just in the midst, and made
a great show as coachman. The young lady
herself was driving, and wore a blue and red
whelk-shell on her head, which was the latest
fashion in hats. She had a profusion of jet
black hair, and a grand embroidered jacket
and dress, but her face was quite red with
anger, as she screamed out to the other
young mermaid,—" *Will* you allow me to
pass, Flora Wavy-Cavey? If not, I shall
call a Shark"—(these are the policemen in
Deep-Sea Town),—"and tell him you're
obstructing the street."

"No more than *you* are," retorted Miss
Wavy-Cavey, with great wrath; "with your
ridiculous big bag. Calling it a *waggonette*,
indeed, and giving yourself such airs on it!
Don't you know you're the laughing-stock
of the place?"

"I don't care if I am," logically replied
the other young lady, whose name was Dora
Willowy-Billowy,—a pretty name, indeed,—
"but I know I'm not half so much as *you*
are. Your sea-horses are the most notorious
old screws in the place, and quite worn out;

I felt quite ashamed the last time you came
to call upon me,—I positively did! And
now, if you don't object, I *think* I should
like to go on."

"You shan't! I won't! It *is* mine; I saw
it first!" screamed Miss Wavy-Cavey, whose
profuse "back hair," comb and all, tumbled
down with the energy of her proceedings,
and sent floating off her smartest new bonnet
trimmed with gold shells, and done up with
the broadest satin-leaf ribbon; and upon
this she jumped up by the side of Miss
Willowy-Billowy, who nearly choked with
indignation, but gave a faint cry of "Oh!"
and "Shark!" and then endeavoured to
settle the matter herself by giving Miss
Wavy-Cavey a resounding slap. This of
course only made matters worse, and they
came to a regular scrimmage, in which Miss
Wavy-Cavey, being the stronger of the two,
seemed likely to get the best of it, when,—
oh! what a shock to their feelings occurred,
—the "clothes-line" became stretched *very*
tight indeed, gave a great jerk, and without
the least warning upset poor Miss Wavy-

Cavey and Dora Willowy-Billowy, the three black footmen and scarlet coachman, all in a heap in the middle of the grandest promenade—in fact, the Rotten Row—of Deep-Sea Town! It then tugged at the waggonette till that surprising vehicle proceeded to sail aloft right up into the very sea above them. "Oh! oh! oh!" they cried, and that was all they could say. It was as sudden and unexpected as an earthquake. And then they all fainted quite away.

CHAPTER V.

MISS WILLOWY-BILLOWY AND MISS WAVY-CAVEY.

WHILE they were still unconscious, Harry, who began to understand matters a little, and to connect the eccentric movements of Miss Willowy-Billowy's new waggonette with the occupation of the charming old gentlemen in the little vessel above, made inquiries, together with the Boots, as to who these young ladies were, and why they were so angry with each other.

The bystanders, who now consisted chiefly of stout old mermen and merboys, and one or two of the wives of the former, informed them that Miss Willowy-Billowy and Miss Wavy-Cavey were considered the belles of the town, and were the daughters of two rich town-councillors, who lived in the handsomest

houses in Coral Grove, and that in consequence there was a good deal of rivalry
between the young ladies; also that lately
a new and mysterious species of carriage
having been seen in the outskirts of the
town, which the chief coach-maker declared
he had made (though it was a "cram"), and
that it was the height of the fashion, Miss
Willowy-Billowy had rushed off and secured
it about five minutes before Miss Wavy-Cavey
arrived at the same spot. Hence the quarrel.
The important fact regarding this "new carriage" was, that it went several times round
the chief streets of Deep-Sea Town, and
paraded in the Rotten Row of the place of
its own accord; and though certainly it didn't
always stop exactly where you wanted to
shop, and sometimes proceeded persistently
to the wrong houses and stood there, yet it
excited a great sensation in the town, and was
considered a very remarkable and fashionable
turn-out. Miss Willowy-Billowy had been
going about in it for a week, and it was supposed Miss Wavy-Cavey had got so jealous of
all the admiration she excited that she stopped

her in the Row to give her a piece of her
mind, and it had led to the outpouring of
wrath, which, as you see, was only checked
by the unexpected catastrophe which has
just been described.

" And a good thing too," said Mrs. Washey,
a bustling, fine-looking merwoman of middle
age. " If I swept out our shop-door, which
you see, sir, is in the principal street,"—here
she tossed her head in grand style,—" I
swept it out twenty times of a morning, in
consequence of that there drat of a waggio-
nette. Such a dust and a dirt! The Sharks
all told me it hadn't ought to have been
allowed,—but there, you might as soon turn
the Sun-fish, as expect sense from that Miss
Willowy-Billowy—a foolish, extravagant
thing, with her new-fangled hats and airs
and ways! A *very* good thing it's gone for
good, and I hope we shall never see *he* no
more."

" *He* " meant the waggonette in Mrs.
Washey's language; and certainly that old
dame had a good deal to complain of.

Meanwhile Miss Wavy-Cavey and Miss

Willowy-Billowy, having had a thorough
good faint, thought better of it, and came
to life simultaneously, rubbing their eyes a
good deal, and fanning themselves with their
pocket-handkerchiefs in a very die-away
fashion.

"Are you better, dear?" asked Miss Willowy-Billowy, who, having lost her waggonette
beyond all hope of recovery, felt more gene-
rous sentiments animate her breast towards
Miss Wavy-Cavey than had reigned there a
short half-hour before. Miss Wavy-Cavey
replied that she thought she was, "but hor-
ridly shaken; in fact, she wasn't sure there
wasn't something amiss with her spine,—
she should see when she got home."

"You know I didn't mean to slap you,"
said Miss Willowy-Billowy, (but she *did* it all
the same,) "only you *were* very tiresome,
and I never mean half I say or do either.
Oh, dear, I wonder what has become of my
beautiful new bonnet that I paid such a lot
for! I believe it's gone up in that dreadful,
horrid waggonette, and I wish I'd never seen
it, and I hope it'll *never* come here again!"

cried she, in a most doleful tone, though leaving everybody in doubt as to whether she meant the bonnet or the "new carriage." Just at this moment a great noise was heard in the promenade close by, and a handsome carriage, formed of a large cockle-shell, beautifully fluted, and drawn by two spirited sea-horses of a gigantic species quite unknown in *our* shallow shores, drew up opposite to the scene of the accident, and a charming old merlady alighted, with an expression of the fondest affection and greatest concern depicted on her countenance; and with a great many " Oh, dears !" and sighings and pantings, folded her youthful daughter Dora to her motherly breast. " I'm so glad I've found you," cried she, rather incoherently; "I heard it all from the baker's boy, whose aunt's mother lives in the top floor of the second house in the street but one next this, and saw it all!—and oh, dear, how glad I am! —and why *did* you go with that queer girl? I always knew she'd bring you to an accident! I never liked her, she was always trying to imitate your best bonnets.".

"No, she didn't, Ma," replied Dora, re-
leasing herself from her dear mamma's arms,
and remembering the slap with some little
compunction; "it was I who did it, and I
believe it belonged to her as much as to me.
Besides, I wish you wouldn't say things *close
by* like this, or Flora will hear, and think it
so unkind."

Poor Flora Wavy-Cavey indeed *did* hear,
but she was accustomed to Mrs. Willowy-
Billowy, whom indeed she liked very much,
as she had once nursed her through the
measles, so that she did not mind particularly, not even when it wasn't true,
which was quite the case as regarded the
new bonnet, as Miss Wavy-Cavey was exceedingly proud of a new style she had invented herself, and which she considered
showed much taste and skill, and the pattern
of which she had in fact, in a sudden fit of
affection, lent to Miss Willowy-Billowy. So
that she was not surprised when that young
lady's mamma turned round and suddenly
said, "Oh, my dear! I hope you'll come
back with us to tea. And if your spine is

bad, we'll put a lobster poultice on, which is an excellent thing, I assure you. My mother used it for twenty years, and then she tried crabs. And now, where are the coachman and the footmen, Dora?" Dora looked about, and soon discovered the three cuttle-fish engaged in a gossip at a public-house close by, evidently describing with great animation the agonizing scene which they had just gone through with their young mistress. "I declare," said one, "I felt as if I were all arms and legs!" To which the merman, who kept the shop, replied, "You don't *say* so!" and poured him out another glass of fresh beer. But she looked in vain for Urchin, the coachman, and his scarlet coat, till at last, happening to cast her eyes on the ground, she beheld him—alas! *him* no longer—reduced to a mangled pink pulp, or, as the mathematical books say, that which has length and breadth, but no thickness. And you see thickness is indispensable to most of us poor feeble beings in this world.

"Oh!" cried she, "take me away, Ma! Give me the salts, Flora! I've sat upon

E

him and killed him by mistake! He was
the nicest, smartest, best Urchin in all the
seas!"

"Oh!" echoed poor Mrs. Willowy-Billowy. "Oh!" re-echoed Flora Wavy-Cavey;
and they all supported each other's fainting.
forms to the carriage, waggling about a
great deal on the way, till they happened.
to hit the right direction, when they fell
all three in a row on the back seat, and
became speechless for five minutes.

"Well," said Miss Willowy-Billowy, after
she had dried three little tears that somehow
managed to fall out of the left corner of her
right eye, "there's one comfort; I don't
think he *felt* it much; do you, Ma? He
must have soon squashed."

"Well, it might have been worse, dear,"
replied Mrs. Willowy-Billowy; "and I've
no doubt everything is for the best. You
remember, don't you, my advising you not
to put on your lilac and green silk skirt,
which would have been quite spoiled with
his pink waistcoat, the colour comes off
so. I must write about a new coachman

for you this evening, and perhaps Urchin's
clothes will come useful. There is no need
to go to unnecessary expense."

The three black footmen sprang at the
back of the carriage, the coachman cracked
his whip, the sea-horses pranced, and off
they went, faster and further till they were
lost in the general whirl of coaches and
vehicles which were going — as if for the
life of them they had laid a wager on it—
in a ceaseless clatter round and again around
Deep-Sea Rotten Row.

CHAPTER VI.

DEEP-SEA TOWN.

HARRY had been so interested in watching the scene that has just been described, that he and the Boots remained rooted to the spot, and scarcely exchanged a word. When it was all over, they could not help laughing, in spite of the accident to poor Urchin, who had been taken into the public-house and was laid out on the table in the best parlour.

"Why," said Harry, "Miss Willowy-Billowy's new waggonette was the old gentlemen's bag that they send down with invitations to the inhabitants to come and stay with them in the ship."

"It shows quite plainly," replied the Boots, "that their language is not understood here. Miss Willowy-Billowy's parcels

and her new bonnet were all they got this
time; and what we saw before seemed to
me to be the 'rag, tag, and bobtail' of the
town: two little urchins of errand-boys, who
were swinging on the carriage by mistake
and couldn't get clear, and a few brushes
and sponges of Mrs. Washey's, that she had
put out to soak opposite her shop-door on
a mat near the gutter. Nevertheless," added
the Boots, reflectively, "of course it will
show they *do* wash down here, and that
they *have* errand-boys. So far, good, though
not complimentary as regards the invitations."

Harry now expressed a wish to take a
walk round the town, and to see some of the
sights, which he naturally thought must be
worth looking at after they had come such
a long way to see them,—like the famous
picture which the rich old farmer went a
thousand miles to see, and which, strange to
say, when he beheld it, appeared nothing at
all in the world but a black something, with
a dingy brown something else in the middle,
and a yellow nose in the midst of that, which

had only made its appearance after a vigorous application of soap and water from some ignorant person who didn't know any better. " Is this the famous picture ? " asked the old farmer. " I see nothing but a nose."

" Look again, sir," said the guide, " and I'm sure you'll see the effect." But the old farmer poked about, and screwed his eye up, and put on his spectacles, and stood on tiptoe, and *still*, do what he would, he could see nothing but a nose.

" It *is* a nose," said he at last, angrily ; " and I believe that's all it's meant for."

" Well," replied the guide, " it may be mostly a nose, too, now I come to think of it; but remember, sir, you've come a thousand miles to see it ! "

Which is a great principle in travelling, and seeing of sights. Now Harry had only come *three* miles, though, of course, that is a long way when it means going straight down in the water, and I think *he* came better off and *did* see something, not only worth seeing, but quite unlike anything he had ever seen before. But before they began their perambulations, a feeling of humanity prompted Harry and the Boots to call at the public-house and make inquiries concerning the untimely fate of poor Urchin, Miss Willowy-Billowy's fat coachman, and to suggest that it might be as well to send for a doctor, to see if there were any remaining sparks of life left in him. To their unbounded astonishment, they beheld the old fellow nearly restored to his natural shape, and sitting up manfully on the table where he had been laid, though he panted a good deal and seemed to have a great weakness in his chest, as might naturally be expected. A doctor was already in attendance, who remarked that he was as well as could be expected under the circumstances, and if it hadn't been the worse for him, it might be the better, only it was better still that it hadn't been worse, as if so, it would then have been the worst thing that could have happened to him,—and showed himself altogether a very sagacious and scientific sort of man. He finished up with remarking, "Handsome is as handsome does," and putting on his hat and top-coat, prepared to leave the room; upon which speech, everybody, including two sharks, the merman who kept the public-house, and his wife and son, applauded loudly.

"What was the matter?" asked Harry, as he jostled past him and the Boots in the door.

"Collapse, sir; case of collapse," said the doctor, without turning round. "I've ordered him two dozen bread-and-milk pills, the size of my fist, which will soon bring him round and fatten him up again. Good morning." And, indeed, poor Urchin *did* seem as if he had taken a good dose of something, for he groaned a great deal and complained of his chest, and declared that his condition was anything but satisfactory.

"I'd sooner," said he, "have stayed as Miss Dora left me. There's always been a family tendency to collapse, and it agrees with us if it isn't too suddint and violent-like, which them nasty bread-and-milk pills don't. None o' them other urchins, as you knows, could get through with this; they're as stiff as boards. I think I'll take a fly home to my cottage." Whereupon the poor old fellow rolled down from the table, and waddled out of the door, patting and rubbing his sides in a most melancholy style, till reaching a cab-stand, he dived into a hackney mussel-shell, and disappeared altogether from the scene.

Harry and the Boots had now leisure to look about them, and observe the many new and curious features of Deep-Sea Town. They noticed, first of all, that the streets were arched over with beautiful pink coral branches, which sprang from lofty stems on either side, and which were ornamented naturally with innumerable rose-coloured spots. It had a very gay and pleasant appearance. The houses were the most picturesque in the world, being grottoes of different sizes, formed of deep blue-and-violet shaded rock, with here and there dashes of rose-colour in it also; the floors of most of the best houses were laid with the many-tinted mother-of-pearl, and the furniture was also entirely formed of twisted shapes of white and red coral. The streets were of the

finest white sand, with golden grains in it
which sparkled very prettily, and were further rendered beautiful by the climbing
sea-plants, which twirled and twisted their
ribbon-like leaves and stalks and feathery
sprays round the coral arches already mentioned.

Then, farther out of the town, whole groves
of the brightest plants and sea-trees flourished,
which waved their broad leaves and delicate
little branches backwards and forwards in
the water with a pleasant murmur, and con-
stituted the home of various fish of all kinds
of colours, which were in a great many cases
the property of the towns-people, who each
kept a small shoal.

From these groves it was that the delicious
spicy odours were wafted about all over the
town, and far above it, which also greatly
added to the warmth and pleasantness of the
water. The mer-people feel these influences,
too, on their sensitive skins, as they are provided with a special sense which we up here
in the upper world don't possess. All this
makes the Deep-Sea country very charming

and delightful. The inhabitants are never at a loss for amusement, as they have so many resources both in themselves and the sea around them to make them happy. Harry and the Boots partly caught the wonderful grace and inspiration of the place, but of course they were not fitted to enjoy it in the same way as its own happy, careless children —the people of the sea.

After wandering about a good deal in the chief streets and the groves outside the town, Harry and the Boots strolled back, to have a last look at the chief promenade before they returned to the green surface of the upper world. One thing struck them as particularly nice, and that was, that all the grottoes being open in two or three directions, while they were still quite sheltered and cosy, made all their owners feel as if they belonged to one family. Everybody was intimate with everybody, even in a way with the people who sold in the streets and swept the houses, and did things of that sort; and they were recognized, too, in quite a pleasant sort of way; and then there was no calling or send-

ing your card or name in when you went to
pay visits. You peeped in at Mrs. Somebody's door, and if she hadn't gone out, and
was there, you immediately entered and invited yourself to tea, and she never looked
to see if you had your best gown on first,
but told the footman to boil the kettle directly.
In fact, it was quite Arcadian. Miss Willowy-
Billowy and Miss Wavy-Cavey were the only
two who tried to upset the simplicity of
Deep-Sea society, and had grand notions of
pretending to knock at an imaginary door,
and inquiring whether any one was in,
when they could see all the while right into
the house, and who was in and who wasn't.
Once or twice Mrs. Merbody, a very sociable
person, who however stuck up for " good old
ways," called out " Yes, I am, but I'm going
out immediately," to snub them ; and so let
us hope that, after the sad upset out of Miss
Willowy-Billowy's "fashionable waggonette,"
they mended their manners and came back,
like sensible mer-folk, to old ways and old
customs.

Harry's and the Boots' experiences of

society were destined to meet with a most pleasant proof of the universal affability before they left the fine old town. As they turned up Coral Grove, they beheld two milk-white sea-horses approaching at a rapid pace, decked with gold harness, and drawing a most elegant yet simple chariot, formed of a pearly nautilus-shell ornamented with narrow lines of gold; and before they had time to wonder who the owner was, it drew up close beside them. Seated in it was a fair young mermaid with a profusion of golden hair, a beautiful complexion, and eyes of the deepest sapphire blue. In fact, she was lovely. She wore a coronet on her brow, and was evidently a person of some importance; but she turned towards them with the sweetest smile and outstretched hands, saying, "You are strangers here, for I know all who live around me. Welcome to Deep-Sea Town! Is there anything I can show you or explain to you in our coral world, which is, I think, quite unlike your own home in that upper one of which I have read? If so, my chariot and my father's house are at your service. He delights in making acquaintance with all who have a love of knowledge and travel, and can in return furnish him with descriptions of things and places he has never seen."

Harry thanked the young Princess—for such he felt sure she was—most courteously, and the Boots made their best bow, but assured her that their time was too limited for a lengthened stay in Deep-Sea Town, which they hoped, however, they should one day soon revisit. The young mermaid then had some further conversation with them, in which she informed them that she was the only daughter of the Mer-king of that territory of Deep-Sea land, and that her name was Ondine, and she the Princess of the land. She seemed at once so winning in her ways and so simple in her plain white robe, quite unadorned save by a light blue belt around her waist and one gold clasp upon her left arm,—the royal ensign of a circling sea-serpent,—and had such frank and courteous manners, that Harry and the

Boots contrasted her involuntarily with the appearance and behaviour of Miss Willowy-Billowy and Miss Wavy-Cavey,—not certainly to the advantage of the latter damsels.

The Princess Ondine was the most refined and intelligent as well as the most beautiful of all the mermaids in Deep-Sea land, and, what was better still, she employed her wits and her means for the good of those of her father's subjects who were in need of her assistance.

Waving her little hand with a pleasant gesture, the pretty Princess bade them good-bye, and drove rapidly away, leaving Harry and the Boots much of the same mind, namely, that this was the fairest vision of Deep-Sea Town, and *quite* worth coming three miles down to behold.

CHAPTER VII.

MR. HERMIT-CRAB AND THE PRINCESS ONDINE.

OUR two friends—I call them two, though, perhaps, you might think them *three*, but the Boots were just like the Siamese twins, and even had the same ideas upon everything, and always spoke with one voice—now began to turn their steps towards High Rock Pinnacle, the loftiest spot near Deep-Sea Town, from whence they intended to start on their journey upwards. As they passed the end of Coral Grove, they heard a loud noise of music proceeding from one of the houses there—a very gay one, by the way, and painted outside all over red and blue spots on a yellow ground; and looking in at the window, they beheld Miss Willowy-Billowy and Miss Wavy-Cavey busily engaged in playing one of the new Fiddle-de-dee waltzes upon a pink-coloured pearl piano, which had evidently cost ever so much. Harry kissed his hand to them, and they immediately rushed to the window and giggled tremendously at him, Miss Willowy-Billowy exclaiming, " Why, it's one of the two-legged creatures from the green world above, I declare ! What impudence ! I never saw one before except in a picture in a book, they come down so seldom ; but mamma used to know lots that were upset out of a thing they called a ship, and came down here and stayed a great while. I wish she would ask him to tea. He looks nice." Upon this, the Boots exclaimed, " I can't let him come in now, young ladies, as his mamma might be anxious about him, and is expecting him back, but we shall hope to send you something very nice from our home in the world above—a new bonnet each from Smith and Jones." But Miss Willowy-Billowy and Miss Wavy-Cavey seemed so astonished at the Boots and their speechification, that they remained standing quite still, as if transfixed, till they had finished

F

speaking, and then they screamed, " Oh, how
dreadful! What a *queer* creature! Did you
ever!" and ran back to. the piano in the
interior as if the sea-serpent had been chasing
them, not seeming in the least grateful for
the new bonnets from Smith and Jones; and
the last Harry and the Boots saw of them
were four white arms whirling away like the
most furious windmills, while the strains of
the ' Fiddle-de-dee ' penetrated every corner
of the Grove, and even made such a dis-
turbance in the water that it apparently
reached towards the far-away habitation of
the Sun-fish, and caused that respectable old
fellow to look as if he had got the quakes
very badly.

Harry and the Boots laughed, and both
agreed that they should like to put these two
lively mermaids in bottles and preserve
them as " specimens "; and while they were
thus discussing their experiences of the
Deep-Sea country, and expressing opinions
on its inhabitants, they quickly approached
the neighbourhood of the peak whence they
were to ascend. Before they had quite

'WHO IS IT THAT IS MAKING ALL THIS NOISE?'—*Page* 67.

reached it, however, they came to a very big "curly-wurly"-looking thing standing by itself at the side of the road, which had a long peak pointing high up into the water, and a large door, over which was written on a board "Science-house"; and when they were quite opposite to it, a very queer, crabbed-looking creature peeped out of the door and said, in a very cross tone, "Who *is* it that is making all this noise? They are disturbing my calculations dreadfully. Just look at the Sun-fish!" He then took off his spectacles and rubbed his head with one of his long claws, and went in again, looking terribly agitated, and, in fact, as if he were bordering on distraction. Voices were heard inside, and presently a most venerable old gentleman, a merman, of course, came out and said, "I'm afraid Mr. Hermit-Crab has been rather rude; but the fact is, he is my Astronomer-royal, and he had nearly calculated how wide the Sun-fish would be if its width were four times less and five times greater than the breadth of the whole, when this shocking organ-grinding nuisance began and quite upset him."

Harry and the Boots didn't like to say that what the Astronomer-royal and the old gentleman mistook for organ-grinding were Miss Willowy-Billowy's and Miss Wavy-Cavey's musical performances in Coral Grove; but on the latter adding "Won't you come in?" they thought it might help to smooth matters down if they accepted the invitation. The old gentleman then turned his back and went inside to lead the way; when they saw that he had a gold crown, pitched, for convenience sake, as it was hot weather, on the back of his head; and a purple robe, trimmed all over with the best star-fishes, tucked up in a bunch at his back. He was evidently the Mer-king and the Princess Ondine's papa.

No sooner had they got inside than they heard Mr. Hermit-Crab retreating up into a passage at the left, calling out as he went, "Well, come up, and be quick about it"; and leaving the spacious apartment,—which was filled with curious instruments entirely new to Harry, all except a cannon-ball, labelled "Meteor," and part of an old

anchor, ticketed up " Stone from a Comet,"
and other little articles,—they proceeded to
enter the door through which His Majesty
and Mr. Hermit-Crab had already passed.
It led into a long passage, with very short
steps, which curved round and round, and
grew smaller and smaller, as they ascended.
and, as the windows were little and placed
at long intervals, both Harry and the Boots
had enough to do to grope their way. It
was most tiring, and they had to sit down
to rest twice; and when at last they did
get towards the tip of this high peak, the
passage became so small that they had to
go on all-fours. This was the principal
reason why the Mer-king had his royal
robes tucked up, though certainly it was
a way he had when he was busy and felt
scientific. At last a flood of light fell on
them, and, looking upwards, they beheld
the Mer-king and Mr. Hermit-Crab standing
on a platform just above, and very busy
looking through a long twisted tube, which
was evidently a species of telescope. They
made room for Harry and the Boots, and

showed them how to look through it, which
they did, and then inquired, as they were
evidently travelled folk, and had passed by
the Sun-fish on their way to Deep-Sea land,
what their opinion was on the structure of
the creature. The Boots replied that it was
a bright phosphoric sort of fish, fed by three
good-natured whales on the choicest sea-
weeds, and always remained stationary in
its home. At this Mr. Hermit-Crab shook
his head and frowned a great deal, and said
that didn't agree with his theory at all. *His*
idea was that it was a spontaneous kind of
comet in the shape of a fish, naturally,—as it
grew in the water,—which was in a perpetual
state of explosion. Probably it would one
day blow up altogether, which would cause
darkness in all the Deep-Sea country, and
kill all the people who lived there in consequence, as nobody could be expected to
live in pitch darkness. This idea seemed
rather to please him than otherwise. He
then directed Harry and the Boots to look
again through the telescope, and see if it
wasn't just exactly as he said. So they did.

Certainly, there was nothing to contradict the theory,—if anybody chose to call the Sun-fish a " comet," it might as well be called that as anything else; but to Harry and the Boots, who had seen the beautiful creature comparatively quite close, it appeared quite different. It looked alive and enjoying itself, and they could see its pretty eyes sparkling as one of the whales, which was almost obscured by its brilliant light, brought it a fresh basket of food.

" There!" Harry exclaimed. " I saw the whale !"

" Fooh ! " cried Mr. Hermit-Crab, in a fume—an expression he always used when expressing incredulity,—" I saw it myself; it was only a passing cloud of sea-weed."

He then commenced a very learned discussion, arguing that no whale could live at such a height; and if it could, it would be too timid to approach the Sun-fish; and if it did *that*, it wouldn't bring it anything to eat; and that if it *did* bring it something to eat,

that proved conclusively it couldn't be a
whale at all. He then made a paste of some
powders, labelled "Logic" and "Inductive
Science," mixing up a little cake, which he
put into a small oven and immediately took
out again, and invited Harry and the Boots
to refresh themselves with it, as it was an
excellent thing when you were busy chitter-
chattering, as they had been just now. Harry
tried it, and found it not of a bad taste, as
he expected, but only half-baked. As he
was trying hard to choke down a particularly
large morsel which Mr. Hermit-Crab speci-
ally recommended, he was relieved by hearing a light step upon the stair, and a silvery
voice, which he immediately recognized, calling out "Papa, dear, aren't you coming home
to dinner?" It was the Princess Ondine;
and giving a little graceful dive at the narrow
entrance, she glided in upon the platform.
The Mer-king rushed towards her, and giving
her a fatherly kiss, inquired "if there was
anything *very* nice, nice enough to entice
him away from his favourite Science-house
and the company of his Astronomer-royal,

adding that she *had* been bold to venture as far as this."

"It wasn't to disturb you," replied the Princess, blushing; "it was only to be in your company." Meanwhile Mr. Hermit-Crab, after giving a sulky bow, had hustled off the remainder of the cakes from the table, and concealed them in a cupboard, against which he sat with his back, as if afraid that the Princess should try to open it, and have a share in the feast. Neither would he say a word, as he considered his remarks and his language altogether beyond the compre-hension of a young merlady, even though a princess. The Princess, who, however, was very amiable, entered into conversation with her royal papa, and Harry and the Boots, whom she recognized at once as the strangers she had met in Coral Grove, and to whom, in his name, she had already given a welcome. They were more than ever charmed with the mingled simplicity and grace of her manners, as well as the intel-ligent way in which she spoke of everything which came under her notice. Harry asked her, in a whisper, if she did not resent the surly manners of Mr. Hermit-Crab, who, on being solicited, positively refused to show her any of the sights of his Science-house, or to allow her to peep through the telescopic tube at the Sun-fish (rather, indeed, to the annoyance of the Mer-king, whose policy it was, however, never to interfere with him); but she replied, sweetly, and sadly, too, as Harry thought, "What matters it, when I shall some day, and, perhaps, so soon, pay a visit to your beautiful green world, and know so much more than we can here. I know Mr. Hermit-Crab is greedy, and does not like me even to see the cakes he makes, although I own he often twits me with never having tasted them,—but let him have his way." Then Harry wondered greatly not at this greed, indeed, for greed is common, but at the fancied value and the false ideas the Astronomer-royal had connected with the poor and scanty productions of his Science-house. And then, for the first time, Harry knew that it was a legend of the Deep-Sea country that all its people should some

day leave that far-down land, and with it
their strange and witching forms, and ascend
to the green world above—his home—there
to walk about, and dwell always as happy
human beings.

CHAPTER VIII.

UP IN THE GREEN WORLD: THE O-FY SCHOOLS.

THE hour had come. Harry and the Boots were fain to leave Deep-Sea Town, and return again through the world of waters to the regions of air; and as they stood upon the little platform, it occurred to them that from no place could they have a better starting-point than from there. So it had e'en come as it ever comes, go where we will—see what we may—to "farewell!" and from the Mer-king and his kindly face, even Mr. Hermit-Crab, and last, not least, you may be sure, the pretty Princess, they won smiles and regretful looks, not unaccompanied by hearty wishes that they would come again, then to pay a longer visit, and see yet more of the manners and customs of the beautiful coral town.

" Stand lightly on the highest point of the long telescope," said the Boots; and Harry and the Boots flew up to it together, and stood poised ready for the spring which they were to make to send them upwards on their long ascent. 'Twas given, and in a moment up they went, with a powerful impulse that drove the waters down beneath their feet, and sent them so far on their way that already Deep-Sea Town and its golden streets, and coral arches and pleasant grottoes, were spread out as in a map before their gaze. Harry took one last look at the group on the platform of the Science-house, and beheld faintly the sour old astronomer with half of his body concealed inside the cupboard, where he was no doubt engaged in consuming Harry's rejected lunch; while the Mer-king sat in an easy chair with his crown on his lap, and wiped his ample forehead with his pocket-handkerchief. And the Princess Ondine? You may be sure Harry looked at *her*. *She* stood at the very verge of the little platform, leaning over a railing which partly supported the telescopic tube; her white robe waved gently about in the waters, her face was upturned as though she were looking after her lost friends; and Harry fancied, in the clear light which shone upon her, that there glittered two little diamond tears in her blue eyes. In another moment she and the Mer-king, and the gruff astronomer, and the Science-house became white and black specks and a dim outline, and then faded quite away.

Up they went, higher and higher; fizz! whizz! rushed the water past them, till they came near the spot where the Sun-fish dwelt, and soon it disclosed itself to them in all its glory. "The Astronomer-royal down there says you're a comet in a constant state of explosion!" roared Harry, with as loud a voice as he could, to make himself heard. The Sun-fish made no reply at all, but looked as if he quite understood it, for he rolled his sparkling eyes round in the direction of Harry, and gave a tremendous wink and smiled. Up they went, still on and higher, leaving *him*, too, behind them in their course, till at last the water seemed to grow thinner

and lighter, and to send them up like corks
with greater and greater force; and the
Boots exclaimed that they were very near
the surface of their own world again. And
before they had time to wonder about it
much more, up they shot right into the
region of air and cloudland again, leaving
the blue sea with such a splash that they
must have looked like a sort of volcanic
fountain.

"Oh," cried Harry, "how *queer* it feels,
and how different it is here!" And then
they travelled with great speed straight in
the direction of the land. They passed over
the little ship still sailing peacefully on her
way, and Harry saw just drawn up with
great toil and trouble Miss Willowy-Billowy's
"fashionable waggonette." They were up-
setting it and eagerly scanning its contents.
"What a beautiful creature," he heard one
of the hospitable gentlemen exclaim; "pray
take care of it." The creature in question
was poor Miss Willowy-Billowy's new bonnet,
with the band-box all crushed in, or surely
they *must* have known it was a bonnet, and

a very smart one too. They crowded around
it, they washed it, they dried it, they made
a house for it, they labelled it with a long
Latin name, and then they sat in a circle
and looked at it, but they *never* guessed that
this was the property of one of the belles of
Deep-Sea Town, and that she had gone to
shop and pay calls in their very own big
leather bag! Half-an-hour more quick
speeding over the foam-tossed waves of the
blue ocean—oh, how fresh the breeze
seemed!—and they caught sight of land;
and flying directly towards it, in a few
minutes more Harry and the Boots stood
once again upon the broad surface of
mother earth.

Oh, how green everything looked!—white
sky and green earth—fields and trees, hedge-
rows and wayside plants, all such a bright,
intense, all-pervading green. Then the
white clouds, pile upon pile in the faint blue
sky, with the sun—*our* far-off sun—clothing
them with silver glory. How different, how
fresh, how *airy* everything was! It was,
compared with the many-tinted coral town

'HARRY AND THE BOOTS SAT DOWN UNDER SOME OLD
APPLE-TREES.'—*Page* 81.

and the heavy-scented sea, just like the difference between a snug warm room, lit up with glancing firelight and bright yellow lights, full of people gaily dressed for a dance or a charade, and a quiet, pleasant drawing-room in early June, looking out on a breezy blue sky,—trees sparkling all over with golden green, after the summer shower, and bending close up to the white-curtained windows,— full of quiet murmuring sound, bird-songs and bee-songs, and summery looks and whispers. Harry was very sorry to leave Deep-Sea land and the dear little Princess Ondine, but he was glad, too, to see all the familiar home-like scenes again. Contented with the mere sight of them, he and the Boots sat down under some old apple-trees and had a good rest. I think they went comfortably to sleep for about half-an-hour.

After they had remained there some little while, the Boots proposed that, as their time was limited, they should take advantage of the present opportunity to pay a visit to the celebrated O-fy schools for little boys, conducted on the Chinese plan, and which

G

were situated on that part of the coast. Harry
asked what the Chinese plan was. The Boots
replied that it meant that they had plenty of
lessons, but never learned any. It was found
to answer exceedingly well, and preserved
good old ways beautifully; and he was
sure Harry would be so delighted with all
their various customs, that he would infi-
nitely prefer it to the stern discipline of
Mr. Coachwell. "However," added the Boots,
" when they got there he would see for himself." So they got up and walked in the
direction of the cliff, along which a very
pretty path led to some fields in which they
soon saw a little building with a very high,
large wall around it. The Boots gave one
hop, and Harry and they perched themselves
on the top of this wall, whence they could
have a capital view of all that was going on
in the enclosure. It was quite full of little
boys, all amusing themselves in every sort of
way; nearly all were in the playground,
which was very large indeed, and surrounded
by the wall, and the rest were in the little
house, reading very hard out of big books, and

doing lots of sums on their slates. Harry naturally thought it was play-time, and inquired
how it was the boys in the little house were
kept in when the others were at play; but the
Boots told him that everybody might always
play if they liked, and that the busy little boys
preferred being in the house and looking at
books, as they had a singular idea that this
was what they were there for. The other
boys thought it was the best fun to learn all
the fashionable games, and know all the O-fy
ways generally, as it was a nice kind of thing
to do. Some grave-looking old gentlemen in
long black gowns walked up and down in the
midst of all this turmoil; but although they
were put out occasionally by the noise, they
were so engaged with reading their books and
talking together that they rarely took any
notice of what went on; and perhaps it was
the best way, as otherwise the very naughty
boys might have been obliged to be thrashed;
and when this *did* occur, it was a dreadful
trouble to everybody. But I must tell you
what Harry saw. He noticed there was a
brook running through the middle of the

playground, and, of course, a great many of the little boys were engaged in dabbling in that. They had several games, but the great one was sailing little boats, and that they were never tired of.

Once in a certain time, so the Boots said, the two best boats were drawn along by the two quickest running boys in the schools, to see which went fastest, when all the boys, new and old, crowded in the playground to see them; and there was such a hallooing and racing, and shouting and excitement, that there might never have been such things as boats invented before. The appearance of the first railway train didn't make half the fuss and noise in the world. Their ordinary ways of amusing themselves, however, were mostly of this kind. Six or eight boys would bring out a table and have their tea—their milk and bread-and-butter together; and when they had finished, they began to sing a number of queer songs, and throw the jugs and mugs about, and sometimes they finished up with smashing the table. That *was* fun !

Harry noticed a little party close to him

and the Boots; they had finished tea, and some had their legs on the table, and some their heads (*they* were asleep), and one got up and sang a song, with his head wagging about a great deal, and looking rather foolish. This was the song:—

> "What a nice little, bright little school,
> It would make a wise man of a fool;
> But fine fellows like we
> Like to play and take tea—
> So we make *that* the rule of our school."

Which they did, certainly. At this there was a great clapping of hands and huzzaing. There were a great many of these teas going on all over the playground, and the warm milk-and-water had made some of the poor little fellows *so* sleepy. Those who weren't at tea were riding about on ponies, driving little carriages, &c., with their caps cocked on one side. They considered themselves the smartest boys there, and wore velvet coats and kid gloves, and smoked the best brown-paper cigars. But that was in the evening, as it was considered bad manners, so the Boots said, to smoke in the day.

This seemed very funny, after smashing up all their best tea-sets; but, as the Boots remarked, the boys were very unaccountable, and as long as you didn't throw your broken dishes and things on the chief walk, where everybody went, nobody minded. But it was quite the thing to behave yourself " afore folk." Peep-shows were also very fashionable amusements in the playground, and a great many of the little boys seemed to have nothing else in their heads. They sat and looked at them for hours in the evening, and spent nearly all their pennies and weekly pocket-money on the men who kept them. And, indeed, the young gentlemen required lots of pocket-money, more sometimes than their papas approved of. One of them, on being asked by his papa, when he had come home for the holidays, what he had been doing that year, replied that he had "smashed twelve jugs, seen a fresh peep-show every evening, and learnt one page of geography." Upon which his papa sent him off immediately with a tutor, who no doubt made him attend better to his lessons. But the time fails me to tell of all the games that were played, and the pranks that were practised, and the pocket-money that was spent by all those little boys that Harry saw; how they used to get outside the playground to race their little ponies; how they used to tie paper tails to the old gentlemen in the gowns; to make bonfires close by the little house, and tease the good scholars inside, besides smashing the windows occasionally, and telling fibs and foolish tales, and getting into scrimmages. All these things they did, and a good many more, till at last the *best* of the playing boys would make a desperate bustle just before they left, and rush to the little house and try to get good marks for their lessons; and no doubt this effort sobered them a little, though it was only to be expected that what came in so quickly at one ear would soon go out at the other.

"Then these," remarked Harry, after they had sat watching the O-fy playground for about an hour, "are *really* little boys' schools?"

"Really and truly," answered the Boots.

"Dear me," said Harry, jumping down from his perch on the wall; "how wise you are! I should never have thought it."

CHAPTER IX.

THE FAIRY FLIRTAWAY.

HAVING occupied their time with the schools during the period that they were resting,—for of course they were naturally tired after coming up such a long distance from Deep-Sea Town,—it now remained for Harry and the Boots to decide what they would like to see next. The Boots mentioned several things it would be desirable to visit, but most of them were a long way from that part of the coast. At last the Boots recollected that there was a very curious little territory some way inland among the mountains where lived a little lady,—a fairy, of course,—who spent all her time catching little boys and putting them in a horrid dark place like a cupboard, but which was built

so as to appear like a nice bower on the
outside. "Would Harry like to see *her?*"

Harry thought he should, especially as
he should like to scold the cruel little lady
and liberate the poor little boys. The Boots
said, however, and rather to his surprise,
"You cannot do that, and, indeed, most
likely she will try to shut *us* up. It will
be great fun, for I'm not a bit afraid of her.
Let her try!"

"How will she do it?" asked Harry, in
some alarm.

"She'll try to bewitch us; but if we take
no notice, she cannot do us any harm. If
we *do*, we may find ourselves, like the little
boys she catches and bewitches, inside the
dark cupboard!"

This idea made the prospect of a visit
to the little lady sufficiently exciting, and
Harry, with a boyish longing for new adventures, proposed they should start at once.

Accordingly, they began to walk—this,
the Boots said, was the best plan in this
country, as you could see the scenery better
—in the direction of some blue mountains

which lifted their lofty peaks before them on the horizon, talking all the way.

"Is she like the Princess Ondine?" inquired Harry, who could scarcely think of any young lady, particularly a fairy, except as being like her, and thought this cruel fay must at least be very pretty to look at, or the little boys would not be so ready to come to her.

"Not at *all*," replied the Boots emphatically, and laughed; "but I can't describe her. She is *more* like the lively Miss Willowy-Billowy or Miss Wavy-Cavey, but more clever than they are."

"Is she clever, then?" inquired Harry.

"Very,"—said the Boots,—"about catching little boys."

That seemed all she could do, or did do; but, as the Boots added, "She does that to perfection, as you 'll see." Whereupon Harry thought, "Oh, foolish little boys!"

They now approached a beautiful valley, which lay between them and the highest mountain, and Harry noticed so many pretty scenes,—trees, church - spires, sheep-

couched in the long grass of the fields, and
gentle spotted cows drinking at the pools
and browsing on the buttercups and clover,
—that he was almost tempted to stay there;
and perhaps it would have been better for
him if he had. But the Boots explained
that, if they wanted to see all the sights,
they must go right on and waste no time
about other things; so they skipped up the
side of the mountain after they had left
this pretty vale, and soon came to the top,
when they gave a great jump down the
whole of the other side. This valley was
equally beautiful, too; it seemed just made
for people to be happy in, and had a variety
of things in it both fitted to employ one's
mind and please one's eye.

The Boots took a little path that looked
as if it were trying to hide itself among the
bushes; but on Harry's asking how it was
he knew the way so well, they pointed to
a little flag, very small, it is true, but on
which was written in distinct characters,
" *My* flag. Come and welcome."

The flag was very gay-looking, and after

it had once caught your eye, you couldn't
help knowing which way to go. Even
Harry seemed to know the direction now,
and they followed the path till it led right
up to a beautiful garden, and opposite a
gateway, over which was a sort of triumphal
arch, and another larger flag flying : nothing
could be more inviting than the appearance
of this little spot. Harry was going eagerly
to advance, but the Boots checked him,
saying, in a low tone, "Hush! there's a
little boy looking in. Let us hide behind
these bushes and see what becomes of him."
So they carefully concealed themselves and
watched, wondering—at least, Harry wondered—what would happen next. For a
few minutes *nothing* happened; no fairy
appeared, there was no noise or sign of her,
and Harry supposed she was not aware that
the little boy was waiting to be admitted.
This, however, was not the case. The little
lady, whose name I may now tell you was
the Fairy Flirtaway, had seen him from the
first, but had not chosen to take any notice
immediately, lest the little boy should be

frightened away; for, though he was fascinated
by the garden and the beautiful flowers that
grew in it, he had heard tales of small boys
being put in the summer-house, and otherwise ill-used, and it would never have done
for the fairy to appear too eager. And she
did not. She looked all round her, hummed
a tune, and then slowly sauntered down her
garden path towards the gate, and presently
cautiously peeped over it.

" What, *you* here, little boy ?" cried she ;
"I had no idea of it "—(this was very wicked
of the Fairy Flirtaway ; only you see this
was the way she caught her little boys);—
" but I'm *so* glad you've come. And I suppose
you want to see my pretty garden, and have
some of my nice flowers and sweetmeats?"
With this she flung open, the gate wide, and
Harry, for the first time, had a full view of her.
She was, indeed, a *lovely* fairy. Upon her head
she wore two blue butterflies, with a pink one
in the middle ; her hair was frizzed so that
it looked like a cascade of golden water,
while her complexion, which was of the most
dazzling hues of pink and white, showed off

to the greatest advantage her pretty features,
which consisted of a little nose which turned
up just a little in the daintiest manner, a
rosebud mouth, and two large innocent blue
eyes over-arched with dark pencilled eyebrows. Then she had the sweetest little
figure, two white round dimpled shoulders,
and little plump arms and hands, and such
little elegant tripping sort of legs and feet,
quite indescribable! The minute you saw
her you felt inclined to go and cuddle her
up like a dolly. To add to her charms, she
wore a rose-coloured flounced skirt with a
gold sash, and from her ears and her
necklace, and her shoulder-knots and her
waistband and sash, there hung lots of tiny
silver bells, which played a kind of music of
the most bewitching kind wherever she went.
Finally, her shoes were made of blue velvet,
ornamented with two large silver butterflies,
quite as pretty as those she wore in her hair.

She *was* a fairy, indeed; you could not
take your eyes away from her. As for the
little boy at the gate, he was so overcome
with wonder and admiration, that he stood

gazing at her with his mouth open, and seemed as if he had quite lost his wits. The Fairy Flirtaway seemed, however, quite accustomed to the sensation she created in the minds of little boys, for she smiled and said, " Shy? Oh, no! Not with *me*. What's your name?—Tommy? Come in then, Tommy, for I must call you so, it's such a pretty name, and you must tell me all about yourself, and see my nice garden."

With this she patted his cheek, and gave him her little hand to help him along and take him the right way; and now Tommy seemed to have gathered so much courage, that he stepped boldly forward with the lovely Fairy, much to her satisfaction.

" None of the little boys," said the Fairy, " who have been here to-day wear such nice coats as you do; and, in consequence, I shall give you one of my best flowers that I am so fond of, which I make a rule never to pluck for *any one*—no, not if they wanted it ever so, and even *cried* for it!"

So she ran lightly to a flower-border close by, all her little bells tinkling and jingling,

and each of her five butterflies on her head,
and shoes waggling and fluttering like life—
it was quite enchanting; and picking the
largest and gayest peony she could find,—
which, she said, showed by its size how
highly she thought of dear little Tommy,
—she brought it to him, and fastened it for
him in the most careful way in the left top
button-hole of his coat. Tommy felt so proud
that he scarcely knew what he was doing;
and when the Fairy said she loved him
better than all the other little boys put
together, and she was sure he loved her, and
that they should be the best of friends,
Tommy declared his intention of staying
with the nice, kind, beautiful Fairy in the
garden all his life, and of leaving his papa
and mamma and his own home altogether!
Upon this the good Fairy squeezed his hand
quite affectionately, and told him he must
take tea with her in the nice summer-house
at the end of the walk, where jam and toast
were always ready, for the Fairy was hospitable to all comers—even her fairy friends
who came sometimes for a jaunt in the

H

garden, and for whom there was a special
table set,—adding, that for *Tommy* she had
had the toast extra well buttered.

"First, though," said she, "you must have
some of my sweetmeats, as they will do you
ever so much good." Accordingly, she ran
to a little box near the path with a handle to
it, " for the convenience of carrying it about,"
the Fairy said, as she rarely went anywhere
without it, it was so useful. It was a fine
box, curiously formed of bits of wood shaped
like arrows, and carefully glued together: on
the cover was inscribed—

> "'Nods and Becks and Wreathed Smiles,'
> Speeches soft and Tender Wiles."

And these were the names of the different
sweetmeats. Tommy was quite eager to catch
a sight of the contents ; and when the Fairy
lifted the cover and took out two of the largest
size, didn't he open his mouth wide and gobble
them up ! The Fairy was delighted, and
called him a " dear, sweet, innocent little
chick " ; and Tommy, who had now become
quite silly, for the sweatmeats being powerful had sent intoxicating fumes right up into

his curly head, immediately called her the "loveliest Fairy that ever was," tottered on his feet, hugged closer and closer to his delightful Fairy in the most confiding manner, and suffered himself to be led up unresistingly to the summer-house, the tales about which he had entirely forgotten. It seemed now, too, more inviting than ever. Over the doorway was written—

" Come, dear friends, and take your seats,
    Here you 'll find the choicest meats ;
    Each of us is like a dove,
    Sure it is the bower of Love."

And the outside presented such an attractive appearance, being entirely overgrown with roses, peonies, sunflowers, and the brightest blossoms of various kinds, that it looked most enchanting.

Just as Tommy and the Fairy arrived opposite to it, she took a small iron key out of her pocket, and waited for a moment pointing out the beauties of the arbour, and describing how jolly the tea was inside, till Tommy grew quite impatient, and made a rush to the door in the greatest hurry, which

the Fairy perceiving, she immediately un-
locked it, and, giving him a push, which might
have sent him along for a mile without stop-
ping in that direction, instantaneously closed
it again with a bang, locked it quite close,
and put the key away in her pocket! She
then marched back again just the same way
she had gone up, as if there were no such
being as poor little Tommy in existence.

Upon this, Harry felt so sorry for poor
Tommy, and so indignant with the naughty
Fairy Flirtaway, that he wanted to go and
let the little boy out, as he felt sure that
even if there were nothing very dreadful in
the summer-house he would feel very lonely,
and perhaps cry at being left to himself.
The Boots, however, told him that it was
locked with a magic key, and that nobody
could help him out, not even the Fairy,
after little boys had once gone in; she could
only put them there: the only way out was
through a dismal lane between two high
walls, without a bit of view, and full of hard
stones, which led far away from the pretty
Fairy and her flowery garden. It was very

difficult to get into, too, and most of the little boys preferred remaining in the summer-house to encountering the perils of the lane, especially as they were always hoping the Fairy would come to them some day, and they could often hear her soft voice.

So Harry and the Boots agreed to wait and watch what the Fairy did next, before they attempted to go to the gate themselves. They had not to wait long. They heard the Fairy singing joyously in the garden, while she planted some fresh flowers, and placed a larger peony than ever in a pot close by the walk; and as she was thus engaged, they heard a sound at the gate, and soon discerned there a very funny little boy, with a large head, and a wise look in his eye, who was dressed up very smartly in a blue velvet coat and knicker-bockers. He seemed, however, a very pert sort of boy.

He stayed at the gate a good long while, peeping, and trying to see what was going forward before he knocked, and was not by any means in a hurry; but presently the

Fairy jingled her little bells so prettily, that
this little saucy boy was rather amused with
it, and exclaiming to herself, " It *must* be fun
in that garden !" gave a loud knock at the very
middle of the gate. The Fairy Flirtaway,
you may be sure, did not give him time to
run away again. She sang one of her best
songs just inside the gate, and then suddenly
opening it, cried out,—" How funny ! I was
just wishing that somebody would come
and talk with me in the garden, it's so
dull to be all alone." (You see, the Fairy
made no allusion to poor Tommy, who was
shut up in the summer-house.) " Do take
pity on me, and come, in and have a little
chat ! "

" Oh, by all means," said the pert boy,
who was besides so conceited, that he considered his presence immensely superior to
any of the quiet amusements of the garden,
which were more than sufficient to interest a
fairy of ordinary intelligence. But I ought
to say here that there was one great pecu-
liarity of the Fairy's garden, and that was,
that nothing could be seen distinctly in it,

except the peony-bushes, the walk, the box
of sweetmeats and the summer-house, and
the little boys who used to visit her. The
Fairy herself could see nothing but these,
and, indeed, to tell the truth, she usually
saw less than the people, whoever they
might be, who came to visit her, always
complaining of the dullness of the garden,
and the bad view from it, and the "nothing-
to-do" generally, whereas there was a beautiful mountain on the right, down whose
azure sides the little streams were wont to
trickle in the sunlight, looking like moving
silver threads, and on whose crest the very
clouds used to come and rest,—clouds so
beautiful, that they seemed carven of silver,
and fringed with light itself,—besides cot-
tages in the village, with many poor people
in them, with very little money, and who
would have been only too glad to welcome
a powerful fairy within their walls, to give
them a little help. Then, too, she had many
diversions in parts of her own garden,—bees
and fountains and birds, and various other
things, which would have amused anybody;

and when you consider that a fairy is able
to employ her time in ways which ordinary
people can't,—to travel far off, and see new
and interesting sights,—without waiting a
moment to consider about it,—I think you
will allow that the Fairy Flirtaway preferred catching little boys to anything else,
and didn't choose to seek for occupation in
other directions. The mist in her garden
which obscured the prettiest objects arose
from her neglect in tending it. But, to tell
the truth, the Fairy really didn't *know* what
to do with her own powers, and was sadly
in want of wise counsel.

We must now, however, record what Harry
and the Boots saw as they stood watching
the pert little boy behind the bushes. They
soon found out, from the conversation between him and the Fairy, that his name was
Master Peter Pickle, and they were much
amused at his little airs as he walked up
the garden path. His manners were a great
contrast to poor Tommy's; and when the
Fairy presented him with the large peony,
which, of course, she said was the first

flower she had ever given to a creature, so far from being proud of it, he began to whistle 'Flowers of the Garden' (which, as I dare say you know, is a very sentimental song), to the tune of 'Ten Little Niggers,' plucking it to pieces all the time, and sticking the petals in a row on his cane, which seemed to occupy his attention more even than the Fairy herself. The poor Fairy Flirtaway had enough to do to keep this little man amused, for he seemed in no hurry to eat the sweetmeats or walk to the summer-house, or to take tea with her, as she solemnly assured him he should do, if he liked, immediately. He skipped here and there, and talked a good deal about himself and his best suit of violet clothes, and his white pony, which, when the Fairy heard of, she made up her mind he *should* be got into the summer-house somehow or other, as, to tell the truth, she had really serious ideas about taking tea with this little boy herself. Peter Pickle, however, winked with his left eye, and said he had an idea that there was at least *one* little boy, if not more, in the

arbour already, adding, that was a thing he
didn't approve of, " though," said he to himself, so that the Fairy shouldn't hear, " not
that I care about that, for if I wanted to go
there I should soon set about it, and keep the
door open too."

Of course the Fairy Flirtaway liked this
boy ever so much more than the others, and
tried all she could do to make him come up
a little quicker towards poor Tommy's quar-
ters. She coaxed him, she scolded him, she
invariably kept her eye on him, and she made
twenty times more of him than she had ever
made of anybody else in her life. The Fairy
Flirtaway always did this. The boys she
was cruel to, and whose little gifts she always
threw about and trod upon, were the simple
little fellows who used to believe what she
told them and were fond of her. Sometimes
one, clever at carving, would spend hours
in the summer-house, cutting her a model
of a little boat,—sometimes another would
give her all his pocket-money, to buy
presents for herself; and they would hand
these things out to her from the windows

of their prison, which were too small and
high to let in much light. And she would
take the little gifts and throw them away
out of sight among the bushes, and never
think of them again. To return, however,
to the particular scene which Harry and
the Boots witnessed; the Fairy and Peter
Pickle had approached nearer the summer-
house at last than that young gentleman
had ever been before, and in an unguarded
moment he stood so perilously close that
the Fairy whipped out her magic key, and
gave a dart at him and a right good tug
almost before he knew properly where he
was. In a second, however, he showed
pluck, and was too quick for her. He
escaped with the speed of lightning round
the corner of the arbour, and from thence
sprang with great agility to the top of the
Fairy's garden-wall, where the last Harry saw
of him before he jumped down was his pert
little head cocked on one side, and his hands
extended in the most horrid vulgar street-
boy fashion from the tip of his nose outwards
into the air just like a spread-out fan—a sign

both pert and impudent. And then, and not till then, the Fairy Flirtaway assumed a haughty mién, drew up her little head, elevated her beautiful eyebrows, and fairly turned her back upon Peter Pickle!

CHAPTER X.

HARRY'S MISFORTUNE.

HARRY and the Boots were so much amused by this little incident, that they remained for ever so long laughing behind the bushes, after which Harry felt so positive that the Fairy Flirtaway was not in the least dangerous to sagacious boys, and that with common caution it was quite easy to escape from her, that he proposed they should pay her a visit in person without waiting any longer. They, therefore, boldly stepped forward into the pathway, and in another moment found themselves standing outside the inviting looking gate. Harry gave a loud knock, and almost immediately they heard a most enchanting sound of little silver bells, and rushing towards her bower-like

entrance, the Fairy quickly appeared, almost
breathless with surprise and agitation.   She
opened the gate wide.   How pretty she looked,
to be sure!   How her little white breast
heaved, and her curly locks waved about in
the wind, and her little bells went jingle!
tingle! with a sweet sound that nobody *could*
describe, but which sent quite a sensation
towards Harry's very heart.   Then she wel-
comed them so warmly, too, and in quite a
different way to the others.   "I never felt
so glad," cried she, with two little tears in
her eyes, and a rosy blush in her soft cheeks,
"to see anybody in my life: and you and
your friends the Boots above all things.   If
you *knew* how I am plagued by the most
tiresome and foolish boys!   I never have a
minute's peace in my garden,—they are always
trying to break into it and play in my summer-house.   It really is *too* provoking!"

Harry felt quite sorry for her now that he
understood things in that light.   Poor little
Fairy!   She went on in the most appealing
manner:—"I have just had such trouble with
a horrid boy who would *insist* on entering into

my arbour : we had quite a struggle ; but at
last," cried the Fairy, clasping her little hands,
" I *did* manage to turn him out—even poor
little, *me!*" (So that was it! Harry began to
think the Fairy Flirtaway was, after all, the
most ill-used being in the world.) " But,"
she added to Harry, " if only some nice sensible boy like you would come and live near
my garden, though *in* it would be better, I
should not mind. I do so want somebody to
come and protect all the walks and flowers I
take such pains with "—(to this Harry could
testify himself); " and you could stay in the
summer-house and have it for your own. I
believe one or two tiresome boys have got in
and injured it, but I could soon turn them
out with your help and tidy it up, for I quite
long to have some nice clever steady boy to
talk to."

At this indirect praise of himself Harry
felt almost, but not *quite*, as proud as poor
Tommy was of his peony, and told the Fairy
he had long been interested in her proceedings, but that till now they had never appeared to him in such a sad and pitiable

light.   He also added, that he had left home
on purpose to make her acquaintance, which
wasn't *exactly* the case, only Master Harry's
imagination, like that of the other boys, was
a little bit excited by the peculiar spell the
Fairy always exercised by her presence.
At this the Boots coughed slightly, but
nobody took any notice.

"Ah!" said the Fairy, "I *thought* there
were some strangers near me, for once I heard
a slight noise among the bushes outside the
gate." And so she had; and being a wise and
cunning Fairy, and reflecting that if Harry
and the Boots had been there they must have
witnessed a good deal of what was going on
in the garden, she determined to receive the
next boys who came to see her, whoever they
were, in quite a different way from what she
had done before.   As they passed the peony
bush, she pointed it out in a careless way,
saying, "That is my favourite bush, which I
planted expressly a week ago for the sake of its
nice crimson flowers.   I even put it into a pot
with my own hands," said she, with quite a
despairing look; "and would you believe it

when I tell you, the boys pull off the blossoms so that I have scarcely one left for myself! *Isn't* it tiresome? See, I believe there's only one poor little bud left!"

And saying this, she flew to her peony-bush like a little bird, and, stooping over it, carefully dusted its poor leaves, and then kissed it, to show how tender-hearted she was, —how fond even of a simple growing plant; and selecting the finest bud from the one or two which still remained, ran with it to Harry, and looked up at him so sadly with her innocent face and her wistful blue eyes, and smiled *so* sweetly with her pretty pouting mouth and dimpled cheeks, that Harry was quite fascinated, and, thinking he had never seen such a lovely fairy before, at once seized the flower with the greatest delight. The Boots gave a violent kick as he accepted the bud, and the Fairy noticed it, saying, "Do your friends the Boots always kick like that?" in such a sorry sort of frightened tone, that Harry felt quite angry with his Boots, and bade them in a whisper on no account to do that again. The Boots wisely determined, therefore, to

I

act the only part left to true friends under
such circumstances, namely, not to interfere
till he got into a hobble, and then to do their
best to help him out again.

The "hobble," as you will hear, was not
so long in taking place. After he had pos-
session of the flower the Fairy had so kindly
presented to him, he became aware, for the
first time, of a strange mistiness around him.
It seemed like a sort of soft dreamy fog, if
one can use such a word to express something a hundred times more delicate in hue
and texture; and everything in consequence
became indistinct except the Fairy Flirtaway, the rising walk bordered with flowers,
and the arbour, which looked somehow more
inviting than ever. As for the Fairy, she
seemed to become positively radiant. Every
moment she grew prettier and prettier, her
dress and the silver bells appeared more and
more wonderful, while her very steps seemed
to have the grace of a fawn and the lightness
of a bird. Then she talked in such an
engaging, interesting way! Never had he
heard such pleasing conversation before. The

Boots might be very wise certainly, but they were ugly old things compared with the Fairy Flirtaway; and Harry now felt rather indignant with them for not having brought him here at once, instead of wasting time down in Deep-Sea Land with the—the—dear me! he had almost forgotten! the mer-people, and the—oh! he remembered her now quite suddenly—the Princess Ondine. Ah! yes, she had seemed to like him, too, but not half so much as this pretty Fairy; and then the Fairy had known so many little boys, and liked *him* best, and preferred *he* should stay in her garden, because he was *sensible*. On the whole, he thought he would say nothing about his adventures in Deep-Sea Land and the Princess Ondine, even though the Fairy, pressed him to tell her all about himself, and especially to tell her if he had ever seen any other nice Fairy or Princess in his travels. "I'm sure you have seen *somebody* very nice," said she, nodding her little head till the pink butterflies looked as if they were going to fly off that minute; "and I should be *so* interested about her."

Harry now began to make himself quite as silly as any boy who had ever been in the garden, and felt, in truth, so vain, inflated, and foolish, that when the Fairy, who soon saw that she need no longer be on her guard, and should soon subdue poor Harry, informed him that she had a fresh batch of sweetmeats of a new kind *expressly* for him, ordered by telegraph from her Paris confectioner's, and produced her box with two beautiful large mauve-coloured and white ones inside, Harry eagerly accepted them. They were now quite close outside the summer-house; and then the Fairy looked so affectionately at him, and told him so tenderly that he could do nothing in the world so well to please her as swallow them both down for her sake, that he took one between his finger and thumb, and was *just* going to pop it into his mouth, as she told him, when, whether the Boots kicked again accidentally, or the Fairy was so much engaged in giving him sweetmeats that she did not see there was a stone in the way, I cannot say, but Harry fell down with a tremendous crash right on the hard pebbly garden path, and lost his sweetmeats, his peony flower, and even the very hat on his head. The Fairy screamed, but never gave him even a finger by way of assistance; poor Harry felt a dreadful pain in his side, and the Boots did their best to help him on his legs again.

When he did so, and once more stood on his feet, he was surprised at the change wrought in that short space of time. It *might* have been the shock of the tumble that cleared his vision; it might have been that the loss of the Fairy's gifts had bewildered his mind; but, at all events, one thing was quite certain, and that was, that things were not as they appeared before. In the first place, the sun had come out from behind a cloud, and the Fairy Flirtaway stood in a spot no longer sheltered by overarching trees, but where the light shone down fully upon her, and Harry was astonished when he beheld her changed appearance. Her rose-coloured flounced skirt was decidedly faded and the worse for wear; her butterflies looked cheap and tawdry; and

the bells which had so charmed his ear with
their musical sounds, he found were made of
old brass thimbles and worn-out children's
toys. He noticed, also, in this intense light
that her hair was false and her cheeks
painted, while her expression no longer
revealed an amiable character, and wore a
winning smile, for there was the mark of an
ever-during frown on her forehead, and a
hard, cruel look about her mouth. In short,
she seemed so completely and thoroughly
altered, that Harry could not forbear exclaiming, "Oh, I thought you were a *real*
Fairy, and you are only like Lily's old doll,
after all!"

And now, indeed, if he had been mis-
taken about the Fairy's intentions before,
he could not mistake them now, as she exclaimed "*Real!*" with a look which might
have transfixed anybody less bold than Harry
or the Boots; and, snatching the magic key
from her pocket, did her best to lock Harry
into the summer-house before he had any
time to make any more observations about
her. The Boots, however, helped him in

this strait, for he was so bruised and bewildered, that he had hardly any strength
left to fight his own battles, and, giving a
great hop just in time, took poor Harry well
out of the Fairy's reach, and landed him
safely on the high ridge which formed the
boundary of her flower-borders. Then the
strange, unaccountable mist cleared away,
and he saw that the same sunshine which
fell upon the Fairy Flirtaway, and exposed
the deceit and trickery of her charms, fell
also upon the purple mountain and the distant scenery, and lit up the silver streams
and rock-crowned summits, and shone upon
the wooded vale beneath with a joyous light,
which seemed full of life and happiness, and
tempted him to return again towards them,
to behold anew their eternal beauty. Then,
too, he gazed down into the garden again,
and saw the flowers that looked so gay
within its borders were artificial ones, and
had no root (as the Boots proved by pulling
up a couple of them and investigating them),
and that they, too, were dingy and faded,
as if they had been placed there in all sea-

sons and weathers. And now, as he glanced towards the summer-house, a rent in the roof disclosed from their high point of view a part of the interior, and they both looked in. It seemed papered with innumerable portraits, nearly all grossly flattering, of the Fairy herself, and beyond that there was nothing—nothing, save a broken-down table, on whose surface reposed the weary heads of three or four of the captured little boys. They seemed half asleep, and half gazing on the gaudy pictures on the walls. The ground was covered with dust and fungus and broken fragments from the roof; and the pretty suits of the little boys—poor Tommy's among the number—were rapidly spoiling in the prevailing damp and rottenness of the place, and on their cheeks were marks of tears. The Fairy gave them nothing—one looked quite thin and starved—except now and then through the window (for she never entered the summer-house herself) a small dish of bruised fruit, strawberries or apples, when she found time to gather them in the garden, and had nothing else to do. And

'I WAS QUITE ANXIOUS TO GET HIM OUT OF THE WAY.'—*Page* 121.

for these the poor little fellows blessed their
"good Fairy," and gave her many thanks,
mistaking it for a feast, and counting those
poor gifts of rotten apples and mildewed strawberries priceless, as misers count their gold.
And there they stayed, having no courage to
brave the freedom of the rough and desolate
lane.   Oh, foolish little boys!

Meanwhile, the Fairy Flirtaway sat down
in a very cross temper by the side of
her garden-walk, at which distance Harry
observed she began to look ever so much
nicer again, and, bringing forth her work-
basket, commenced to sew up a number of
fresh butterflies for her shoes, which was
evidently one of her chief occupations.
Harry heard her say to herself as she plied
her needle,—and let us hope it enlightened
him completely, as to her regard for him,—
"I wish that stupid boy hadn't tumbled
down in *my* garden.   I shall have to tell the
gardener to roll the walk again, as, of course,
I don't like it to be untidy.   I'm sure he
must have seen I was quite anxious to get
him out of the way before anybody else

came!" And upon that she stuck, at least,
half-a-dozen new butterflies on her head for
ornament, and brought out a pot from her
green-house, this time with peonies in it as
big as cabbages, which she looked at with
great satisfaction. Just as she had finished,
another knock was heard at the gate, and off
she tripped to it, leading in presently, with
a smile sweeter than ever, *two* little boys,
who were evidently bent upon going straight
to the summer-house, and whom she kept
one on each side of her, and talked first to
one and then to the other. As Harry gazed
into the road outside, he saw several more
still coming, attracted, doubtless, by the gay
flags and the triumphal arch (though many
of a more serious and sensible disposition
passed by); and without waiting to see the
fate—no doubt a cruel one—of the boys
within the garden and the boys without,
Harry and the Boots, with one accord, gave
a tremendous hop and leap, and soon reached
the fresh pure air, and trod on the soft
elastic turf of the mountain summit.

"Ah!" exclaimed Harry to the Boots,

with whom he was now on the best of terms, and evidently forgetting the part he had lately played, "what an absurd Fairy that is, and how *is* it she manages to lock up all these poor little fellows?" But the Boots replied, "Nay, rather, what foolish little boys! As the Fairy says, ' They *will* come to my gate and crowd into my garden, and help to spoil it too; and if they are so *very* ready to drink tea in the summer-house, they must take the consequences. Of course, I know that I have a magic key to let them in, but neither I nor anybody else can open the door again and pull them out.'"

It seemed to Harry rather a heartless speech of the Fairy Flirtaway; but then, as the Boots remarked, fairies were expected and encouraged " to behave as sich," and it was, undoubtedly, perfectly just and true. So Harry began to inhale with as much pleasure as he could the keen exhilarating breeze on the high mountain-top, and never said a word to the Boots about the pain he still had to a great extent in his left side!

CHAPTER XI.

THE BREEZE AND THE CLOUD.

THEY sat quietly on the mountain-top for a long while, and as it was very lofty they had an excellent bird's-eye view of the surrounding country. Of course, they naturally talked a good deal about the various sights they had seen, and the Boots made a good many wise observations upon their last adventure and the Fairy Flirt-away's garden.

"She would have been a dear little thing," said he, "if she had only been a little less vain and had dressed sensibly, and if the boys had kept out of her garden. On the other hand, the boys would be ever so much better, and would never get into such trouble and spoil their best clothes in the dusty old summer-house, if they hadn't been extremely foolish and conceited, and greedy about the flowers and sweetmeats."

" But why," inquired Harry, " does the Fairy seem to take such delight in catching little boys ? "

" For fun," said the Boots. " She likes chasing them in her peculiar way; and it's for just the same reason—fun—that the boys think her garden so delightful."

This seemed about the true state of the case, only, as the Boots explained to Harry, it was a pity for others besides foolish little boys, as in the ideas of people generally it gave rather a bad name to fairies on the whole, and they didn't get helped in important matters as much as they ought. In fact, it had come to be considered rather funny if you were a sedate fairy, and didn't set up a garden and try to catch boys. Though, as the Boots remarked, " When you properly *considered* it, nothing was more really unfairy-like than to use your magic powers in such a foolish way; adding, " that these were things which people might see in time when they thought about it more. At present they didn't make many inquiries on the subject."

Nothing could be more pleasant than their seat on the summit of the beautiful purple mountain, and on all sides were views so extensive and delightful, that they scarcely knew which to admire most. The Fairy Flirtaway's domain in the valley beneath had dwindled into a green speck, quivering with the hot air and moist vapours, from which, on this breezy height, they were entirely free. All things were spread out as in a map before them—hills, plains, towns, villages nestling in their white orchard bowers, placid blue lakes and winding streams, which on the West became one broad and flowing river, rolling onwards in the distance till it reached the mighty sea. And there, a long way off, ships with bright sails glided peacefully on its dim blue horizon, some coming to the towns upon the coasts, others outward - bound. Harry could see all the world.

Nobody would have guessed that Deep-Sea Land and its coral groves existed, and its countless inhabitants dwelt merrily beneath that placid surface. But as the Boots said, "Who would ever think there were such strange things, and so entirely different from each other, to be seen here on the land?" Each village, they told Harry, had something to show quite of its own, but it would take far too much time to visit them all. If they did, Harry "would never get home in time for tea."

"Ah!" said Harry, "I must not forget my promise ; but I have still several hours to spare, and in that time we can go a long way if you take some good big hops!"

I should tell you that in all these countries one hour was as long as several of our days, and yet the time was so accommodating, that when you got home, if you had been ever so long away, the clock in *your* house had perhaps only gone on for about five minutes. This was because all the clocks in the new countries were taken care of by a very useful lady, called Miss History, and she always made *her* time go to the furthest, and stretched it out a great deal. It was a very good plan,

and in consequence anybody who went out
where she presided over them could easily
get home in time for tea or supper, as the
case might be.

The Boots now pointed to a large enclosed
piece of land a good way off, with a number
of buildings in the middle of it, with fine
towers and pinnacles, as well as Harry could
make out for the distance, and asked him if
he wouldn't like to visit that country and see
the famous town of Chattermuch.   As the
Boots said they were the queerest people in
the world who lived there, and could do what
nobody else could, as he would see when he
got there, Harry replied that he thought he
should.

"Well, then," said the Boots, "I needn't
trouble now to take any more hops.   We
have only to call a cloud and go."

Accordingly, they looked over the steepest
side of the mountain, which seemed to lead
down into a dark ravine, and, catching
sight of a small cloud, taking its case a few
yards beneath, spoke to it, and said they
wanted to take a journey to Chattermuch

Town. The Cloud seemed rather stupid, but said that it knew the place very well, only he must speak to the Breeze first, as if he didn't happen to be going that way it would be very inconvenient. Whereupon the Cloud stayed quite five minutes whispering with the Breeze: no doubt trying to make a bargain, for as it stepped up on the summit it said, "that in consideration of the travellers being Harry and the Boots, the Breeze had consented to do it cheap." Harry and the Boots thanked the Cloud cordially, and leaping elegantly into the midst of it, made themselves comfortable for their journey. The Breeze gave a shrill whistle among the grey crags and boulders which stood boldly forth from the green turf of the mountain-top, and without a moment's loss of time they fled faster than they could have imagined from their pleasant resting-place.

"I had no idea," said Harry, "that clouds flew about so quickly. I always thought they were peaceful, quiet, silly sort of things."

K

"Thank you," replied the Cloud, who, of course, overheard, "all the same; clouds couldn't travel very far without a brisk Breeze to push them on. Ours is a noted one, which never travels at less speed than forty miles a day, and always goes in the same direction. He's as steady as an old coach-horse."

"Ah!" said Harry, "it's delightful!" And it was. They had such a view all over the country, and then the Cloud had such nice soft cushions for them to rest on, and went along so smoothly, that it seemed more like a *dream* of travelling than anything else. No noise, no fuss, no bustle; no turning in and out of crowded carriages, and losing first one's luggage, and then one's-self, as is the fate so often of us poor travellers in our little railway trains. It was all quiet, gliding motion, and soft repose, and dream-like rest, while the green fields and trees below flew backwards with a rapidity at which Harry was astonished. In fact, he enjoyed his journey so much that he became quite sorry when it drew to a close; and when the Breeze, slackening its pace little by little, allowed them to drift gradually on to a huge cloudbank, such as you may have seen piled up in the sky on a sultry day when thunder is muttering in the distance. It had no life, such as the little clouds possessed, but merely supplied the material from which they were formed. Often had Harry wished to fly off to a beautiful golden-tipped cloud-pile to see what it was like, and who lived there; and now, there he was!—his wish gratified—as one's wishes are sometimes when one does not in the least expect it. Before, however, he had time to take even a glance at the new scenes around him, the Boots thanked the Cloud and the Breeze, saying, he supposed they "would be always handy if they wanted them again, and that they hoped the former would take the opportunity of amusing itself with its companions."—(of whom there were several in a crowd together, all apparently belonging to different persons and families in the city), and then immediately gave a great spring down to the far-off

ground, and landed Harry just opposite
an ancient archway in a high thick wall,
something like the great wall of China, only
it wasn't kept so well, as there were lots of
weeds growing on it.

It was the wall surrounding the city of
Chattermuch, which had been built by one
of its oldest kings in former times, the king
Sayadeal, who was a very wise, nice sort of
man, and did his best to protect the town, of
which he was justly proud. The gates were
evidently kept closed against new-comers,
which was, of course, a very proper arrange-
ment, as otherwise it might have made a
good deal of confusion in the town, and
obstructed the traffic of the inhabitants, to
say nothing of enemies, who might do much
worse mischief. There was, however, a bell
conveniently situated on the ramparts, with a
rope to ring it, so that anybody who made
noise enough was sure to be able to get in
sooner or later.

Over the door was carved the beautiful
legend, "Nothynge butt conversationne is
spoke Here," with a most elegant bell and

clapper sculptured on a knight's shield for the city arms. Our travellers gave the bell on the ramparts a resounding peal, and patiently awaited the result.

CHAPTER XII.

HOW HARRY AND THE BOOTS STORMED CHATTERMUCH TOWN.

AFTER the last echoes of the big bell had died away,—which took time, as each separate tower of the city expected to have a voice in the matter, and kept up its own peculiar echo in great state,—Harry heard a noise overhead, which soon manifested itself as two voices engaged in hot altercation. Presently one voice exclaimed, "There, I told you so—foreigners! And very queer! They must on no account be let in."

Harry and the Boots looked up, and saw a fat little man straining to peep over the parapet at them, which exertion served to make him rather red in the face, and a good deal more cross. When he saw that he was

perceived, he exclaimed, " Oh, bother! don't
look at me like that!" and disappeared.
They thought this was rather uncivil behaviour, and were debating whether they
should take the town by force, and skip
right over the wall,—which would have been
quite as bad manners on their part,—or
abandon their idea of seeing it altogether,
when another very fat and still redder face
looked over the parapet at them, smiling,
and a most *suave* and courteous voice said,
"Never mind *him*. Would you like it in
the ' Court Jumbler ' or the ' Fashionable
·Cackle'? They're both excellent periodicals,
and will be published at five o'clock."

The Boots laughed, and Harry replied
that he really " didn't know what the gentleman meant." " Oh, I mean," said that
personage, who had overheard the remark,
" the news of your arrival,—of course. The
fact is," he went on, " our royal Sovereign,
the King Chit-Chat, who is the most agreeable person in the world—you must be introduced to him to-morrow—is always so
delighted to hear all the news, that he offers

five new sixpences to anybody who will bring
him the *newest* piece of news; and the consequence is, we get such a quantity of news
generally, new and old, good and bad, that
we don't know what to do with it. The
town gets quite full occasionally, and has to
be cleared out. But it 's only to make room
for more. In consequence, we know such a
lot here,—you 'd be surprised.—The individual I was talking to just now—rude creature, wasn't he?—was only trying to get
the start of me,—gone off to put you in his
muddling paper, the 'Chattermuch Turntides';
but I 've '*done*' him capitally, as I have set
up a room for printing the latest editions of
the 'Court Jumbler' here—inside the gateway;
and one's just been sent to the king himself;
so I shouldn't wonder if he were to invite
you to dinner immediately. Saw you coming
by express cloud, with my new electric
telescope, which *does* magnify,—in fact, it
made you bigger than I see you are in
reality. Wonderful thing, isn't it? I don't
know what your names are, but I put 'Extraordinary Probable Arrival of a Gentleman

'HE IMMEDIATELY GAVE A SHRIEK OF DELIGHT.'—*Page* 137.

and his Boots.' Well now,—ah! where
was I? Oh, you see that's why I and the
other fellow were quarrelling. By the way,
what *are* your names?"

At this he looked so eager and interested,
that Harry was foolish enough to tell this
voluble little gentleman, who immediately
gave a shriek of delight and flew off, his
feet clattering inside on the stone steps of
the gateway tower with such a noise that
you could hear it half a mile off.

" Well," said the Boots, " if you hadn't
been quite so quick, I would have told you
not to say anything till the old gentleman
had let us in. I expect we shall have to
stay here for about an hour till he comes
back."

And so they had, as Harry found to his
cost, for he was tired and hungry, and naturally wanted to get to his journey's end,
and not to be kept waiting hours outside
town-gates, while people were talking about
him. During that time one or two more
sober-looking persons than they should have
expected after this, came to the walls at

different parts, and looked at them through their eye-glasses, making various remarks as ideas occurred to them. To judge from their looks, they seemed rather disappointed. One said, " Well, you know, it's quite clear the young gentleman hasn't got boots as big as haystacks." To which the other replied, with his head on one side, his eyebrows elevated, and an air of crushing wisdom and importance, " Ah, you know, these things depend on climate—on climate. I have been persuaded of that ever since I had an opportunity of witnessing its effects on a great-aunt of mine,—(bother these weeds, how they sting!—the Town Council ought to take it up)—most extraordinary thing you ever saw—" Upon which he began to tell a long tale, with a great deal of strutting backwards and forwards, and his hands under his little coat-tails. Evidently the " great-aunt" was so well known that nobody listened; but then that doesn't matter at all when a person is very much engaged about himself; and long before it had come to its proper conclusion, a great panting and puff-

ing was heard in the gateway-tower, and the
civil, fat little old gentleman in another
moment put his head over the parapet,
mopping his face, which was redder than
ever, with a yellow silk pocket-handkerchief.

"It's gone!" cried he. "Oh, dear!—express
edition to the Palace. And so—oh! bless
me—so you're still here. I thought you
might be gone. Well now, that's a remarkable occurrence, I take it. 'Great Sitting
of the Young Gentleman called Harry and
his Boots outside our Tower-gate for more
than an Hour!' Looks well, doesn't it? Yes,
I must, indeed—return in a minute, you
know—it is quite worth while!"

So saying, he flew this time in a breathless
condition from the wall, and again they
heard his clattering boots echoing far and
wide—once more they were left alone; and
there fell again around them an utterly
doleful silence.

Harry thought he was mad, and began to
be quite in despair; but the Boots said,
"The best way to get into this town is to
hop right into the midst of it. I'm sorry

now we landed outside the wall and went in for politeness, as there is always this tiresome delay for travellers."

"But why," asked Harry, "don't all the inhabitants come and look at us, and take more interest in our arrival, as there seems such a fuss about it going on inside ?"

"Because," replied the sagacious Boots, "it isn't their way. I can assure you that when we are once inside-the town they will take very little notice of us. What they are so much occupied with are their own conversations, latest editions, and the king's bounties,—in short, the *news* of us, but not *us* at all."

Harry thought this very funny. Being of less consequence than one's own news seemed something like being of less importance than one's own shadow; but the Boots assured him it was the custom of the town, and everything so far had certainly gone to prove it.

"Now," said the Boots, "though it *is* bad manners, we'll give a hop which will land us right in the centre of the city."

Harry willingly agreed, and in another second they had flown high above the wall and the provoking gateway-towers, and had dropped gently down on a grass-plot in front of the finest buildings there. In the portico, which was very grand indeed, with gold pillars and much carved work, stood a handsome old gentleman, dressed in the most extraordinary style in gold and tissue-paper.

He had a gold crown, pantaloons, stockings, and shoes, and a crimson waistcoat; and then he had a flowing robe, with twenty capes one over the other, like cabmen used to wear in rainy weather, made of the most silky tissue-paper, in different colours, and ornamented with printed things all over, which, however, it was impossible to read, as it was in the smallest type, and all mixed up together. In fact, he was all gold inside, and tissue-paper outside; but, notwithstanding his curious costume, his manners were so pleasant, and his bearings so graceful and high-bred, that Harry instinctively began to like him.

"Well done!" cried he, on seeing Harry and the Boots fly down in the centre of his lawn. "Very good. Now," turning to six-and-twenty footmen, each with a trumpet and banner, who stood near, "you had better let the papers and the people know—they like it."

And, accordingly, the six-and-twenty footmen ran off as hard as their legs could carry them, blowing their trumpets at a tremendous rate, and, in fact, rousing the whole town.

"Yes," said his Majesty (for, of course, this was the King), looking thoughtful for a minute, "I dare say you're surprised at the way we do things here. But you will soon get accustomed to it, and, I must say, with some pardonable amount of pride, that we are the first city in the world for news! Think of that!"

Harry was only too delighted to find somebody who could even imagine he and the Boots *were* surprised, as it looked hopeful; and the King went on to say, "Now they will be as busy as bees, measuring the leap, and so on; but, never mind, come in and have a chop, and tell me all about yourselves, for if old Mr. Busybody's latest editions were correct you have been a long while outside the gate of the town. I really thought of coming to fetch you myself," added the kind old King; "but there, you know, a king can't always 'do as he likes— should have spoiled old Busybody's little game." Here he laughed and nodded, and exclaimed, "There you see—they're at it again."

Harry looked round and beheld crowds of people advancing in the direction of the lawn, with Mr. Busybody, the active editor of the 'Court Jumbler,' at their head, and furnished with scientific instruments and measuring-lines. One of the twenty-six footmen now came running up to say that the rest of the townspeople had gone with the cross personage outside the gate to take measurements there, and that when the investigation was completed they meant to celebrate the occasion by a grand dinner at the Town Hall, at which it was humbly

hoped his most gracious Majesty would
condescend to be present. As for Harry
and the Boots, nobody, except the King,
took any notice of them at all.

The King said he should be very glad, if
he had finished his chop in time; but as soon
as he got inside the Palace he assured Harry
he would sooner have a chop a yard square
to eat than go to one of their dinners. "*Too
fatiguing*, you know," said he. "Pooh!
tish!" (this Harry found was a favourite
exclamation of his Majesty when excited),
" very good people, very fond of news; but do
bother immensely!" With that he skipped
upstairs with the agility of a schoolboy, and,
throwing open a door, displayed the dearest
little room in the world, with a table covered
with a gold and white cloth, and covers laid
for three, and flying to an easy chair, threw
his royal form into it with so much energy,
that his long tissue-paper robes and his
twenty capes made a noise equal to half-a-
dozen steam-engines.

"Dear, dear!" said he, "I'm afraid I've
mixed up the last court poem with the ac-

count of the ' Rise and Progress of Chatter-much Town.' Can't be helped. Must get a new gown." And then he ate his chop with zeal, and bade Harry and the Boots eat theirs too. The Boots sat on a chair and ate heartily. Harry ventured to ask him why he wore a robe so liable to get crumpled and " mixed up," to say nothing of its being so likely to tear, and also why it was printed all over with what children call " reading."

" Why, upon my word, "I don't know," said he, " unless it's because they're so anxious to tack everything on to me. I talk to 'em, you know, back,—in exchange,—and that pleases the whole town. I've a hundred and five old robes, all torn to rags with wear-ing, and so on, because I'm not like a person that can stay in one place and sit still for the sake of my clothes, and of course there's not much that can be done with them now; but nobody seems to mind, and so I don't. Pooh! Oh, no! old robe—why should they? I dare say they'll mend and make up nicely for Seraphina."

Harry inquired who Seraphina was, and

L

the old King said, "Well, she's my niece,
but she isn't often here. She was so fond
of news, that she went out to Otaheite to
see whether the black men played the piano
well, and I haven't seen her since. Remarkable girl. Hope she'll turn up some day.
Talking of young people, however, reminds
me—you *must* see my adopted children; they
are a show; in fact, they make as much noise
as half Chattermuch Town put together."

And rising up, the hearty old King, who
was determined Harry and the Boots should
have a full view of all the sights in that
celebrated city, walked briskly forth and led
the way.

CHAPTER XIII.

WHAT THEY SAW THERE.

THE King, and Harry and the Boots had not proceeded very far from the Palace before they came to a large open square, with a great ladder set in the midst of it, which reached right up into the huge pile of clouds which Harry had noticed on his first approach to Chattermuch Town.

Crowds of people were constantly ascending; and as he looked up he caught glimpses here and there of numbers more, comfortably seated in various parts of the cloud, which certainly looked soft and inviting, and was situated some considerable height above the ground. He could only, however, see so much of the inner side of the cloud as rents in it occasionally disclosed. It was a most curious spectacle. Harry couldn't help inquiring of the King why so many people went there, and if there was any view or other attraction to induce them to take the trouble to ascend the long ladder.

"Well! as for view," replied his Majesty, "I can't say there is much, unless you get near one of the peepholes, which often get filled up. But it's convenient: if anybody overworks himself with talking and so on down here, he goes directly for a change of air to the cloud, and it's wonderful how well it agrees with him. We all go there more or less, and it's surprising how comfortable it is. Quite charming!"

Just at that moment they passed under a dark cloud-patch, which was very much smaller, and was almost isolated from the large one; and while Harry was wondering with all his might what there could be so very delightful in a cloud which evidently never went anywhere and had no view, like the smart little cloud-coach they had arrived in, he heard a most melancholy but distinct sound of a voice proceeding from it, while the little cloud was violently agitated, till at last a pair of black legs, the feet of which were cased in a pair of very untidy old slippers, were seen poking through. Immediately after a noise was heard, something like the squeaks of a tin flute; but, oh! how melancholy the squeaks were; and then the voice sang to a most doleful tune the following song:—

> "O dear! the cloud is full of damp—
>   O dear! but weeds are on the wall;
> Yet sitting here gives me the cramp,
>   Alas! why was I born at all?
>   *Chorus.* Alas! why was I born at all?"

Then the voice sighed "Heigho!" deeply, and commenced again:—

> "O dear! the town's a dismal spot,
>   The nettles sting upon the wall;
> Yet cold and foggy is my lot
>   Up here! Why *was* I born at all?
>   *Chorus.* Alas! why *was* I born at all?"

The Boots laughed, the King took out his pocket-handkerchief and wiped his eyes, and Harry exclaimed, "What *can* he mean, and who is he?"

"Well," said the King, "it's Mr. Two-Rhymes, the town-poet. I'm sorry for him, but what *can* I do? He *will* sit in that horrid little black cloud, and he *won't* come down, not even when I told him I'd ordered ducks and green peas for dinner! I can't help thinking people must like it, you know, when they go so far as that," added the King, reflectively, for ducks and peas were his favourite dish; "but it sounds uncomfortable, don't it?"

By this time the poet had just finished singing a third stanza, and ended with a more doleful wail than ever, "Alas! why was I born at all?"

"Nobody asked you to be, I'm sure," said a pert damsel, with a bonnet stuck all over with flowers, a pink and blue dress flounced to the waist, and twenty streamers, of different shades of ribbon, flying from her chignon, who was just then ascending the ladder with sprightly steps.

"No, they *didn't*," said the poet, in an ill-used tone, and, tuning up his pipe, he sang in as melancholy a strain as ever:—

"They never asked me why I came,
They never told me where to go;
Indeed, I think they're much to blame,
I only wish I'd told them so!"

The pert damsel had by this time disappeared in the cloud, and was, no doubt,
occupied with her own affairs; she *didn't*
trouble herself much about the poor poet;
and the King, who had been obliged to use
his pocket-handkerchief several times, now
called out, " Come, come, Mr. Two-Rhymes,
don't take on so. You know, if you *will* sit
in that nasty black cloud—I'm sure it casts
a shadow over a third of the town—you
can't expect to be cheerful. But I wish
you wouldn't! It would be so much better
for you and everybody else too, if you'd
only come down. You want new slippers,
too. Come, and I'll take you to the new
shoe-shop; there's one opened next door to
the Palace."

But even this inducement—you see the
good King bethought himself of everything
that was most attractive—produced no result.
The melancholy poet swung his two black

legs slowly backwards and forwards, began
tuning up on his flute, and then remarked,
in a quavering voice, that "he should be'
ill if he came to live in Chattermuch Town."
To which the King replied, in a whisper,—
for he didn't wish to hurt his feelings,—that
"he thought he was ill now"; and they
then left the poet's neighbourhood.   The
last Harry "saw" of him—if you could say
so—was the little black cloud in a greater
commotion even than before, and the two
attenuated legs of poor Mr. Two-Rhymes
swinging up and down in a more melancholy
and helpless way than ever.   He couldn't
help asking a question or two about him,
however, and so he inquired "Why the
weeds prevented him from coming down ? "

The King thought that it must be "because poets were more tidy than ordinary
people,"—and there certainly seemed no
other answer.

"What 's he like ?" asked Harry, who felt
some pardonable curiosity about an individual at once so miserable and so determined
to be so.

"I really don't know," replied his Majesty; "the last time I saw him he wore a wig; but that's ages ago. He said it had the effect of increasing one's wisdom very considerably. We never see anything but his legs, as the rest of him is always in the cloud. Perplexing, isn't it?" added the King, whose heart had evidently been touched by the sad case of Mr. Two-Rhymes.

Harry and the Boots both remarked that the people in the large cloud seemed very happy and contented; and the King assured them everybody was so who went there, and that in consequence some people insisted on living there pretty nearly all their lives. "The Lord Mayor has gone there," said he, "as well as the Minister of Inland Works, and the Town-Crier, and they won't come down except just now and then to get through a little chattering. Rather a nuisance, that." Harry thought it must be too, and, lifting up his voice, in a very high key shouted up to the people in the cloud, and asked them "what they saw there?" Two or three heads looked through a rent, one of them belonging to the

pert damsel who had made the saucy speech
to the poet Two-Rhymes, and two others to
gentlemen unknown to Harry, but which the
King recognized as belonging to the Lord
Mayor and the Prime Minister, who had just
left Chattermuch Town the week before. They
all replied that they saw ever such a deal;
but as their views were quite different, Harry
understood it must refer to scenes in the
cloud, and not real views of the world beneath.   The young lady with the ribbons
said she saw four beaux, all extremely handsome, and with large purses in their pockets,
and she didn't know which to choose; while
at the same moment the Lord Mayor cried
out that he saw a most stylish portrait of
himself, with a coronet on his head, robes,
and a gold wig, and a pigtail; and the Prime
Minister was sure he was sitting in a bower,
with a peal of bells ringing in his honour,
and a board put up with "Universal
Spring-Cleaning—the Prime Minister did it!"
thereon, and, in short, they were so full of
these various things, that they immediately
disappeared, and a great noise of talking,

exclamations, and descriptions of all these sights could be heard, in which evidently at least a score of voices were engaged. But as the King told Harry and the Boots, it wasn't the least use staying there to talk with people who were in the cloud, as not only did they see altogether strange sights and totally different from anything below, but it was tiresome to shout so much, as they were really a good way off—farther than they looked. So they went on, the King, as usual, pointing out any objects of interest he thought they might like to see, and asking them numbers of questions about their travels. I have not recorded them, as they would become tedious; but the good King asked at least a thousand questions, and obtained a variety of information, which he seemed to be extremely delighted to have, although he did not in the least know what to do with it. One scheme, however, had thoroughly taken root in his mind, and that was, to dig up old Primitive Prim, pyramid and all, and send a deputation straight off for him to Rory-Tory Island.

Harry told him it was a long way off, and, for all he knew, the island, which was isolated and no doubt volcanic, might have entirely disappeared; but nothing would satisfy the old King but an attempt to bring him to the town, at all events; and calling Mr. Busybody, who was passing, to him, he told him he must really exert himself and endeavour to fit out a body of capable persons to undertake the mission, the expense of which he meant to defray himself.

Mr. Busybody said, in his usual way, "If your Majesty really means it—why, really—yes, a capital idea! It will add a whole supplement to the 'Court Jumbler'!"—upon which he ran off to devise a "latest telegram" of his ideas, the King's, and everybody else's upon the subject. It was singularly lucid. As this took time, the King despatched three competent gardeners, with pickaxes and shovels, and an active gentleman, to find Mr. Busybody, which, when they did, they tugged him forcibly to a vessel in the small river outside the city wall, and immediately set sail for Rory-Tory Island.

Poor Mr. Busybody felt acutely leaving his little printing-room and his electric telescope in the gateway-tower, and uttered many a heart-searching lament; but consoled himself at last by exacting a promise from his brother that he would peep through the telescope for at least three hours before he was expected to return, and on no account allow the 'Chattermuch Turntides' to report the first intelligence of him. After this business was finished, the King recollected his adopted children, and said they might as well have a look at them now, though he was afraid most of the clever boys were gone.

"They do a little work," said he, "for the town and for me, such as potting flowers, mending boots, patching clothes, and so on; but they spend most of their time blowing trumpets, talking, and, in fact, making a confounded noise. I'm told it's a good thing by everybody, and certainly nobody minds, or I'm sure I should not allow it. But it's quite part of the show, so to say."

And so, indeed, it seemed. For, taking a few more turns, they arrived at one of those

grand buildings, the towers of which showed
so conspicuously in the distance (the next
grandest belonged to a rich merchant, who
kept hunters, with mother-of-pearl saddles,
and had silver dining-tables, and altogether
spent his money very usefully indeed, being
quite happy as long as he was the town's
talk); and from thence proceeded such a
clamour, as with all its noise they had never
yet heard in Chattermuch Town.

Passing under an elaborately sculptured
archway, they entered a small chamber,
beautifully decorated with statues, stained-
glass windows, scrolls with poems of the
poet Two-Rhymes, and so many fine things,
that Harry was quite astonished. He was
still more so when they reached the apartment, or rather hall, whence the noise proceeded, and saw about a hundred boys,
dressed in the most costly fashion, and sitting each side of a long table covered with
letters, tea-pots, tea-cups, sausages, and a
number of things, which altogether made
something very like a " litter." " I thought,"
said Harry, " from what you said, that these

were clever boys you had engaged to do your work; and they seemed to be playing at a game, and also to be dressed as if they were very rich."

"So they are," said the King. "No poor boy, however clever he was, could possibly gain admittance into this fine building, as every one of these boys who live here has paid a bag-full of new half-crowns into the bank for being allowed to come. It's considered a great honour, I suppose, because the hall is so fine, and the rich boys do all they can to come here. They liked to be asked to the Palace, to the best children's parties, and to see their names in the papers. And as the soldier-boys and the sailor-boys, and the rest, run off with all the other grand buildings, and the prizes in them, why, it's only fair, I suppose, the rich boys should have a chance of living in a nice large house, with a hall where they can play about, too. You see they are playing their favourite Fox-and-goose game."

"What is that?" asked Harry, who noticed that the boys were far too busy with their

sports to notice them, and only recognized
the King by taking off their caps and putting
them on again. " They only seem to scuffle
about a good deal."

" The two boys sitting at the top and
bottom of the table," explained the King,
" are called foxes, and the rest of the boys
on each side call themselves the geese. And
when a goose wants to do some work,—mend
the town-pump, for instance,—he tells all the
rest of the boys what he is going to do, and
the boys on his side of the table back him
up, and the boys opposite scream, and try
to prevent him, and throw orange-peel at
him; and if he shouldn't be able to fetch in
the pump with all this opposition, why, it
would have to be left outside."

" But suppose," said Harry, " the pump
really wanted mending ? "

" Pooh — tish — hem ! " said the King,
greatly disturbed ; " I declare I don't know.
The boys don't look at it in that light !
Perhaps the town tinker would patch it up
for the time somehow, but it's hard to say.
The foxes are always trying each to get boys

over to his side of the table, and they're knowing old boys, I can tell you."

"It seems to me," said Harry, "that they wouldn't do the work if it wasn't for the game, and that they wouldn't play the game if the building wasn't so grand."

"No doubt a great many wouldn't be bothered," replied his Majesty; "but a hall lined with red velvet *is* nice, and a table spread with perpetual tea and muffins is not a bad sight. I don't come here as often as I used, but when I do, except for the noise, I find it very amusing. Sometimes they come to such a quarrel that they have pretty nearly all to be turned out, and fresh boys come in. That's when the leading fox-boy can't get his way about something, and turns cross. It's a pretty game," added the King, reflectively; "and, considering that the work for the town is very stupid and interrupting sometimes, very well played."

One of the foxes and his party were now all of them engaged in throwing orange-peel, and, I am sorry to say, even sausages and weak tea, at one poor little fellow who was

M

trying manfully to exhibit a new kind of
broom to sweep everybody's door-steps, and
which at last he was obliged to put away
in the great cupboard; and amidst a tremendous uproar of cheering, hissing, and
screaming, which quite filled Chattermuch
Town, the King, Harry and the Boots went
out.

CHAPTER XIV.

PRIMITIVE PRIM'S NOSE IS PUT OUT OF JOINT.

HARRY felt rather relieved at getting into an atmosphere of comparative quiet, and the Boots, who had hitherto made few observations on account of the good nature of King Chitchat, who did all the honours, now observed that as they had seen one or two of the principal sights of Chattermuch Town, though not by any means all of them, it would be better to leave, as they could easily pay another visit to it. But the good King would by no means hear of it, as he said he particularly wished them to be present on the arrival of Primitive Prim, if the deputation succeeded in digging him up; and he hoped they would help him to entertain the old gentleman, as he thought it must have been dull for him in Rory-Tory Island, and all he wanted evidently was a good rousing up.

In consequence, the Boots advised Harry to stay, which, on the whole, he seemed very willing to do, as he was a wonderful fellow for seeing everything, and enjoyed King Chitchat's company exceedingly, he was such an easy-going, gentlemanly, kind-hearted old man. They were all on the point of returning to the Palace to rest and refresh themselves, when they heard a tremendous noise in the direction of the town-gate, and looking towards it, beheld a vast crowd of people all talking at the top of their voices, which were pitched at a very high key. Harry could not hear what they said; but presently one of the King's footmen came running up to say that the deputation to Rory-Tory Island had just returned, and that "they were fetching the gentleman in the pyramid from the vessel in a wheel-barrow, and everybody was reading out loud about it in the papers," which, of course, accounted for the noise. Several other

persons also came with the news; and last
came Mr. Busybody's brother, with the 'Court
Jumbler,' and also the editor of the 'Turntides,'
each of which journals had two extra sheets,
which they had been so busy printing that
this was the reason they had been delayed.
They both came up breathless and in such
a hurry that they fell on all fours, and a
mischievous breeze, which saw how it was,
made the papers fly out of their hands into
a pool of water, so that nobody could
read them !

The King smiled, the two gentlemen got
up, looking very doleful and rubbing their
knees, and on observing the accident to the
beautiful editions of the 'Court Jumbler' and
the 'Turntides,' were so affected, that they were
obliged to sit down on a seat which happened
to be near and dry their eyes with their
pocket-handkerchiefs. Upon this, the King,
who always encouraged the praiseworthy
zeal of his subjects for the public benefit,
sent for the town beadle and bade him fish
out the poor bedabbled papers from the
puddle, when they were immediately des-

patched to the royal laundress to wash and
iron, and dry on the clothes-horse in the Palace
kitchen; so that these two excellent persons
were comforted, and the King was not
disappointed of sooner or later having
his news.

The King now gave orders that the
deputation should bring Primitive Prim
straight off to the Palace and make him
comfortable in the courtyard in the interior,
which was nice and sandy; and he didn't
feel sure whether Mr. Prim would like to go
in his sitting-room, though he quite hoped
to persuade him eventually; and, accordingly,
the footman ran off in high glee to say that
" they was to wheel him directly to our
house." The footman always talked of the
Palace as " our house," and was very proud
of it. And then the King, Harry, the Boots,
and the two editors, who were anxious about
their papers, all flocked together to the
great quadrangle in the centre of the King's
Palace. It was a nice large convenient spot,
with a fountain at one end, a grass-plot in
the middle, and a clothes-line at the other

end, with the King's stockings hung out on
it, of which, as they were not his best ones,
there was a large variety, all of different
patterns, as it was washing-day at the
Palace. The chamber-maid had just hung
a grey pair up, with blue and yellow spots on
them; but they did not look to advantage
just then, as they were very much attenuated
by the wringing-machine, and looked as if no
legs could by any possibility get into them.

" We'll stand here," said the King, turning
his back on the stockings, which sight he
did not much relish, as everybody knew
whom they belonged to, and, somehow,
wrung-out stockings don't add to one's
dignity; so everybody else turned their
backs too, and pretended they hadn't seen
anything but the fountain, and didn't know
there was such a thing as washing-day in
the world. That was true politeness. As
for Mary Ann, the chamber-maid, she hung
up two pair more, out of spite, exclaiming,
" Well, if ever! Of course, if the kitchen
clothes-horse is all full of rubbishy papers
and things, the stockings must go somewhere,

and I hope that'll be a warning to him,
I do!" Whereupon she went in, appealing
to cook in great wrath.

However, the King and his party had not
long to wait at the fountain (which was not
particularly amusing, as it had run dry the last
week, and the King had to send round to the
gardener to turn it on), for a loud rumbling
noise was presently heard, accompanied by
a sound of many footsteps, and before they
had time to turn round, the deputation,
accompanied by at least a dozen persons,
advanced through the entrance towards
them. Mr. Busybody came last, wheeling
a large wheelbarrow, and supported on each
side by two stout workmen, and they were
all red in the face, and puffed and panted so,
that it was evidently as much as they could
do to get along. When, however, he had
arrived opposite the fountain, he let down
the two handles with a great bang, and
nearly upset poor Primitive Prim, who had,
indeed, been dug up, much against his will,
pyramid and all, and now presented a sorry
spectacle to Harry and the Boots, who had

seen him in his isolated grandeur in Rory-Tory Island. For the poor old gentleman gave an audible groan, and appeared very unhappy indeed. The groan, however, came from the very centre of him, for, alas!—it was *quite* true—Primitive Prim was curled round and round like a catherine-wheel, with his head in the middle and his feet on the outside, and appeared rapidly approaching some fearful climax in his existence. He had hollowed out a large cavity in the top of the pyramid, upon which he rested as comfortably as anybody could who was in such a dismal plight; and what with the journey, and the shaking about, and the annoyance of being dug up, he evidently had reason for groaning.

"Bless me!" said the King, "but you don't mean to say he has been always in that condition?"

"Oh, dear, no!" replied the Boots; "when we saw him last he was sitting up in a rational posture. Perhaps he's angry at being removed."

"Yes, I am," squeaked poor Primitive

Prim, in a muffled voice, from the middle of him; "they had no business to do it. But that's not it. I'm beginning! I said I should! And I shall be more venerable than ever now! Oh, dear!"

"Tish—pooh!" exclaimed the King; "let's look at it! Dear me. It *is* an individual, I declare,—who'd have guessed it? I say, old gentleman, don't you think you had better think twice about it? Can't go on in that way, you know."

"Yes, I shall," replied Primitive Prim, curling up tighter than ever; "I wish you wouldn't tease me so. Can't you see that I am endeavouring, as hard as ever I can, to become a Fossil? One would think you had no sense at all, any of you."

"Ah!" said the King, putting up his eye-glasses, and poking at poor Primitive Prim with his stick; "but you know you're as soft as ever. Don't you bother about it! I expect you've seen one of those curly-wurly things they find in the rocks, and it's gone up in your head!"

"It's no such thing!" screamed old Mr.

Prim, in a rage; "I know what I'm about.
I shall be the biggest fossil in the British
Museum when you're nowhere, and I hope
you will be too. I never knew such stupid
people!"

On hearing this audacious speech applied
to royalty, Mr. Busybody exclaimed, "'Remarkable Impudence of the Old Gentleman
from Rory-Tory Island'—excellent article!"
and ran off, puffing, with renewed energy, to
his sanctum in the city-gate, muttering, as
he went, that "that was all it was worth,
and that he'd had enough of the old party."

The King, however, laughed immensely,
and, turning to the two stout workmen, who
now expressed their opinion that "he were
a curious warmint," proposed that they
should uncurl Primitive Prim by force.

It would be quite impossible to describe
the wrath of that venerable old gentleman
on hearing such a shocking and wicked idea
uttered in his presence. He shook with rage,
and declared that the first person who came
near him he would kick black and blue; and
as his feet were still free, it had the effect of

preventing the two workmen from approaching him for a few moments.   The King, however, gave a wink, and promised, in a whisper,
sixpence apiece to the two men if they would
undertake it; so, before old Mr. Prim could
say another word, one of the men had seized
his boots, and the other his arms, and were
doing all they could to pull him out straight.
They found it was harder work than they
had imagined, as old Prim, who had the
strength of a young lion in spite of his
being so venerable, curled up again as fast
as they undid him, spluttering with anger
and exclamations the whole time.   Just as
everybody was beginning to wonder who
would hold out longest, the wheelbarrow
gave a sudden and unexpected lurch, and
rolled out poor Primitive Prim with an
impetus which sent him right along the
gravel-walk to the fountain, into which he
tumbled with a terrific splash before he had
even time to cry "Oh!"   Oh, what a splash
there was! For the fountain had been in full
play for quite ten minutes before!
    This was an ordeal which even *he* couldn't

'A VERY DOLEFUL FACE ALL SHINING WITH WET APPEARED OVER THE EDGE OF THE FOUNTAIN-BASIN.—*Page* 173.

stand very long; and before the King, Harry
and the Boots, the workmen, and everybody
else had recovered their wits and run off to
see if he was quite drowned, a very doleful
face all shining with wet and a long
draggled beard appeared over the edge of
the fountain-basin; and as soon as they lent
him a hand, Primitive Prim crawled out,
dripping with water, but still bent like a
bow,—and, throwing himself upon a little
grass-plot which was near, in a very weak
way,—lay there as if he were nearly done
for.

As soon as he had recovered his voice, he
said, " My nose, as you see, is quite put out
of joint! And, in consequence, I am afraid I
shall be obliged to give up the idea of being
a fossil."

And his nose, in truth, with the shock of
the tumble, and the concussions he had ex-
perienced along the gravel-path, was, alas!
bent quite on one side; and, as it had been a
most venerable-looking feature, it was a very
sad accident.

The King, however, who never *could* understand science properly, or why it was nicer than anything to be a fossil, exclaimed, "That's right! Never mind your nose; I'll tell John to fetch a bath-chair for you, and you must come in and have some dinner. I have some excellent toddy in the cupboard, and I am sure you must be hungry."

Poor Primitive Prim replied meekly that he thought he was, now he recollected it; and in a few more minutes Harry and the Boots had the satisfaction of seeing the poor old gentleman wheeled away into the Palace in a comfortable cushioned bath-chair, which must have been pleasant for his old bones after all, as he never once looked round at the pyramid. Shortly after the footman came out to order it to be brought in, as "the old gentleman, who," as he said, "ain't such a bad fellow, after all, leastways rather eccentric in his manners, was a-going to lecture on it after dinner, and liked to have it by him as a relish." Perhaps he meant relic.

And that was the last they saw of the little stone pyramid and Primitive Prim.

CHAPTER XV.

SHADOW-LAND.

HARRY and the Boots took one more stroll around the town, hearing, as usual, a great deal of talking, and the most talking generally about nothing in particular. One thing amused them, however, very much; and that was, a very funny, fat man, who had a remarkable property of expanding like a soap-bubble, and who, accordingly, caused much inconvenience to his neighbours. All the celebrated wise men—the logicians—had been to see him, as it was quite against their laws that a person could be in two places at the same time, and they could make nothing of him. One of the wise men, who lived next door to him, had, indeed, brought an action against the fat gentleman for occupying his garden without lawful permission, as the latter had made a bet that he would be in his own garden and his neighbour's at the same time,—which, indeed, he was, and broke down the fence as he expanded into it.

There was a great chatter about it, and of course a great deal of quarrelling; but the judge decided that the stout gentleman had better in future keep within his own garden, while the wise gentleman would do well to move his house in case of accidents, as it was a bad thing having such a weak fence between oneself and such an eccentric and unaccountable neighbour. " There is no saying, you know," said the judge, refreshing himself with a cup of tea after his speech, " where he might go to next. It's a serious thing."

And everybody thought what the judge said was uncommonly good, only the worst was that after all the same thing might happen again any day, unless the whole of the stout gentleman's family were provided for in a large garden by themselves,—an island would be best,—and never had any neighbours. Harry and the Boots couldn't help laughing; but they had little leisure left them to linger amidst the many scenes of Chattermuch Town : it was time for them to return to the Palace and bid the kind old King farewell. As they approached the grand entrance which they had noticed on their first arrival in the city, they saw King Chitchat standing within the portico as they had seen him before, only on this occasion he no longer wore his royal robes, but a flowing dressing-gown, with fifteen beautiful tassels at the bottom of it, which made even that look quite handsome and regal, particularly as it was made of purple dimity covered all over with gold sprigs. When he saw Harry and the Boots, he shook hands with them most cordially, and, on hearing they were going to leave immediately, expressed great sorrow, and ordered a large beef "pasty" to be brought from the larder at once, in order that they should be well provided with something to eat on their journey. The Boots inquired after the health of old Primitive Prim, who had now

N

been for many hours within the comfortable Palace; and the King replied that he had eaten the leg and wing of a goose, with pudding after, and though rather weak on his legs and rambling in his discourse, was, on the whole, as well as could be expected under the circumstances. And then, with many expressions of regret on both sides, our travellers and the King bid each other good-bye, and in another moment, by the aid of a most vigorous hop of the Boots high into the air, they had flown over the city wall, and found themselves once more outside the fair domain of King Chitchat, the beautiful and enterprising Chattermuch Town.

It seemed very silent—something like you feel after leaving the parrot-house at the "Zoo," or a great room full of machinery, but, nevertheless, it was pleasant; and the Boots proposed that they should fly away from this part of the world now, and lose no time, as mamma was expecting him, and it was getting nearer tea-time than ever. So they flew away once more, right over the big cloud which hung above the busy town,

and into the midst of which Harry was now
fully able to look, seeing many people
indeed, but to his astonishment no beautiful
scenes such as they had described, and
nothing like them, only woolly cloud, and
nothing more!

He asked the Boots how it was, and the
Boots explained that when people went up
into the cloud they always saw lots of
pleasant sights which nobody else did, and
that was why they were so fond of going
there. "It doesn't in the least matter *your*
not seeing them!" said they, laughing;
"people always have nice visions who do
nothing but sit in a cloud, and I suppose
it's a sort of reward for the pains they take
in going up the ladder to get there. It may
not be a useful occupation, but it has wonderful attractions for the people of Chattermuch Town."

Harry was rather mystified, but consoled
himself with munching at a corner of the
pasty which he had tied round his neck
with a piece of string to save trouble. It
was excellent, and helped to put him quite in

good spirits. The cloud vanished out of their sight, and with it the last faint outline of the city towers; and on they went, and then mountains rose between them and the plain they had left—beautiful dark blue mountains, whose great crags were smitten by the golden sunbeams till they shone with answering fire, and down whose grassy or heather-covered slopes peaceful sheep nibbled and the wild deer sprang; and these, too, were left behind, and still they sped. Many other mountains did they pass, too, with valleys between and wide plains, till at last the sun sank beneath the horizon while they were still travelling, and the light became soft and subdued, and they no longer saw things as clearly as they had done before. They went on still, till they came to a land where was no house nor city, and where no man lived, and where it seemed as if nothing could ever break the peaceful silence.

This gentle spot was folded in amongst the blue hills, and therein, in the midst of the valley, reposed a lake so calm and smooth, that it seemed to exist only to mirror the stars which paced onward in the sky above, or the moon who peeped down on it over the side of the nearest hill with her sad and thoughtful face. The lake ever received with tender love into her bosom those images of peace, and Harry saw and loved her still waters, when he and the Boots flew softly down and stood quietly upon the pebbly shore.

So they stood in this strange and silent land.

For a moment they spoke not a word—the spell of silence fell on their spirits with such potent influence; and then the Boots whispered softly to Harry, " This is Shadowland!"

" It seems a sad name. I don't know why," replied Harry, with a sigh; " I am sure I have never been here, but somehow I seem to have seen it before."

And a tiny breeze came across the lake without ruffling its placid face, and rustled almost inaudibly among the bending rushes by the shore, saying, with an answering sigh, " Yes! you have been here before!" and then it held its peace.

Harry did not seem surprised that the
breeze spoke to him; in the stillness that
reigned on all around everything had a voice,
and a more eloquent one than ever he had
heard in gay and busy Chattermuch Town.
The silent voices of Shadow-land,—the fairy
spirits of Fancy and Memory and Beauty,—
could not be heard *there*. But they were the
reigning fairy queens in this sad and peaceful land, and though Harry saw them not, he
felt their influence, for they hovered perpetually around him, and touched all things with
their fairy wands, so that in their silent way
they, too, spoke. Nor did Harry inquire how
and when he could have been here before,—
it seemed rather a time for resting and thinking than for asking questions; and he and the
Boots being weary, sat them down on the soft
grass—almost grey in the twilight—close to
the pebbly shore. As the evening hours stole
on, the moon, as was often her wont, crept up
beyond the dark forehead of the largest hill,
and, looking down on the Lake, saluted her
with sad eyes, but a gentle smile. The Lake
replied, " So you have come! Bring out the

Stars!" and smiled too. And as she spoke,
here and there stepped softly into the blue
realms above the Moon's attendant maidens,
each with its finger on its mouth and noise-
less tread. Yet it seemed to Harry as though
they sang, and he asked what the song was;
and the Lake and the Moon and the Stars
answered, "Hush! the Evening Hymn!"
And this they chanted till the Moon had
stepped high up into the vault of heaven.

CHAPTER XVI.

THE BEAUTIFUL SHADOWS.

Now when the Moon had reached a place whence she could look down on all the scene beneath her, Harry was able to see more clearly all that was around him. The dark enfolding grey hills, the deep blue Lake, with its border fringes of long rushes, the sloping shore, with its round white pebbles and mossy banks, all displayed themselves with a soft distinctness that the blinding broad white light of day rarely bestows. Nor was this all, for I have said that this land was peopled with rare shadow-beings, who came to you if you would listen to them and show you cared for their company, but never could be sought. As Harry sat quietly on his moss-grown seat, he thought he heard a whisper in the air, and, looking upwards, beheld a young maiden clad in grey, with a bright star on her forehead. So strange a being was she, that you could see through her form,—the Lake glistened through every fold of her soft garment,—yet she spoke in such a voice as Harry had never heard yet in all his travels.

"You have come a long way and seen all the world," said she; "tell me, have you seen the one who loves me? He is always searching for me, but I cannot go to him."

Harry replied that he had not, and tears glittered in her eyes; but the Boots replied, "The one who sought you knows now that you can never be found till he comes to live here in Shadow-land, and he has wedded another not like yourself, and thinks no more for the present of the 'old likeness that once he knew.'"

The pure Shadow-maiden wept and stole noiselessly away. The Boots did not tell her that though her faithless lover had thus forgotten her fair form, his gaiety and his forgetfulness rarely made him glad.

But before they had ceased to think of her, the light semblance of a child danced towards them with apparent joyousness of heart, till Harry saw that it, too, was clad in grey, and had, in spite of its curly locks and fair round cheeks, a mournful expression, such as no child ever wore at play. The star, too, glittered on this little one's forehead. It was the sign of an immortal nature, and was worn by all.

"Tell me," said he, "where my long-lost companion is—the one I used to play with? He went away so long ago, and he has never come back. Where is he?"

Harry again said that he knew not; but the Boots answered, "I saw him not so long ago, in a busy city, poring over large volumes, at a desk, in a close narrow room, where the sunshine rarely comes. He often thinks of you."

"Ah! cannot you bring him here?" cried the little Child-shadow, with a wistful look. "I feel forgotten, and I am so lonely!"

"He will come to Shadow-land sometime soon," replied the Boots; "and then, be-

sure of it, the first thing he will do will be to
ask for you."

The Child-shadow looked more hopeful,
but seemed as if he saw a shining vision
that was a great way off, and while that light
still shone in his eyes, a sudden flash like a
shooting-star startled them, and a strange-
shaped being, with a pale green body and
rosy-red eyes, all radiant light, flew towards
them, and cried, "Ah! these are *my* domains,
you know; we must be gay, we must be
merry, in spite of it all; come my Shadows,
come and dance!"

And his eyes twinkled, and the strange
being skipped and whirled about and sang,
and finally danced again a wild weird dance
among the rushes.

"Who is he?" asked Harry, more
alarmed than pleased at the antics of the
little gentleman, who seemed half mad.

"They call him Will-of-the-Wisp, sometimes, but he has another name, 'The Light
of Joy.' His home is almost always here,
though once or twice he has danced into the
outer world. People have tried to secure

him, and to hold him fast, but they never can, he so rarely comes and is so swift to go."

And as he spoke, Mr. Will-of-the-Wisp fled into the middle of the Lake, and danced there on the water without causing a breath to stir its placid stillness; and his wild bright rosy reflection, contorted in a thousand ways, contrasted strangely with the pure white reflection of the pale-faced Moon.

" Always merry," whispered the Lake, dreamily; " don't you know that this is only Shadow-land ?"

" Nevertheless," said Will, " it is more real than half the world yonder. I have been in it once or twice, but I could not stay! I longed for my companions the Shadows, and was not happy there."

" Tricksy sprite!" exclaimed the Moon, " you are too unstable."

" Perhaps I am," replied Will; " but still this is more my home than the big world, and I must stay here. Where are all my playmates? Come and dance!"

And as he spoke there stole from secluded nooks among the mountains—their quiet

'BUT THE SHADOW HAD GONE.'—*Page* 189.

homes—a hundred flitting Shadows, each different, yet each lovely in face and form, and crowned with the glad star on their foreheads. One, surpassing most in his exquisite grace of shape and countenance, danced past Harry and the Boots with footsteps so swift and light, that they could scarcely discern his course, —how he came or where he went. Harry could not forbear uttering an exclamation, and said to the Boots, " It is so beautiful, that I must follow it! He must come with me and live in our world."

But the Shadow had gone.

And the Boots replied, " That beautiful Shadow often pays visits there. He comes to the chambers of the poets and the studios of the painters, and they entreat of him to remain with them, sometimes with tears, that they may welcome him with their sweet songs, and paint him in fair colours, so that he may be seen and remembered in our world. But he never stays! Before they have time to talk to him, he is gone elsewhere, or else back to his home in

Shadow-land. He is one of the few Shadows who can wander so far, but he stays but a second, and then he flies away."

So Harry saw that it was useless to pursue that swift Shadow-spirit of beauty, which was so fleet-footed that he could not follow him with his eyes, and so strong that he never grew tired.

"It makes me sad," said Harry, "to see them here, and all alone. The little child, —see, there he is, dancing with the others in the very centre of the Lake,—he is not happy, for he has no other Child-shadow who loves him, and would play with him. He seems all alone."

"He is the childhood, the boy companion of the young man in the busy city; and now that they are separated, they can never meet again till the young man leaves our world, and comes through here on his way to another land filled with beauty and goodness."

Then the Boots told Harry that all the Shadows were sisters and brothers of the human beings in the world that he knew,

but that they were of such unearthly beauty,
that they could not live there any more
now, though one or two did come sometimes. "When a human being sighs," said
the Boots, "he thinks of Shadow-land; and
when he sees something lovely that he cannot describe, or feels sad, he scarcely knows
why, it is because a Shadow has been for
a moment standing near him."

"Why cannot the Shadows live any longer
in the world," asked Harry, "when they
could make people so happy by being always
with them?"

"Because," answered the Boots, "the
hearts of the human beings are not wholly
good. The Shadows love them, and therefore they live as near as they can to them,
but they can rarely speak to them; and all
they can do is to stay in Shadow-land till
the glad day comes when they can meet
again, and go home happily together. And
then they will cease to be Shadows clad in
mournful grey."

"That's a long while, I think!" said
Harry, with a sigh.

" Yet it will come!" replied the Boots.

For a long time they rested there on the soft moss-banks close to the white-pebbled shore, and looked on the wild fantastic dance of the Shadows, which, led by the playful Will-of-the-Wisp, sped in sweeping circles over the still surface of the Lake. Not till the Moon became sleepy, and told them she was going to bed in her old corner behind the furthest grey hill, did they desist. Mr. Will-of-the-Wisp, who was always pert, threw a bulrush at her face, and exclaimed, "That he never knew anybody who was so perpetually in the dolefuls;" but the Moon took no notice; and as soon as she had tied on her night-cap, which was made of a dark purple cloud, she took a sudden dive, and was soon out of sight and asleep. The Lake, who was fond of her, became very dull and gloomy, and shone no longer with bright smiles and light glances. Her great companion was gone, and she felt alone. Therefore, she was sad, and said not a word. The Breeze, however, had more than ever to say for himself, and roamed about

here and there in his restless, fitful way,
busy about nothing, yet speaking with a
tender, low voice, which was sweet and
musical. He came up to Harry and the
Boots again, and said, " Still here! Why do
you stay? Don't you feel melancholy? The
Lake won't talk to us, and the Moon is
gone away."

Harry replied that he thought he *did* feel
melancholy now that the Breeze reminded
him of it, and asked him " if *he* ever left
Shadow-land and came into the great
world?"

" Often," answered the Breeze; " but this
is my home; and that is why, when I sing
in the pine-tops and whisper among the
fresh green leaves of the aspen-trees or the
elms, that I make people sad. I remind
them of Shadow-land. But *you* are not
obliged to stay here, you know; indeed,
I was surprised to see you, as I knew you
were one of the beings belonging to the
great world. Nobody but the Boots could
have brought you, and you are here before
your time. There is work for you to do

o

there, and you must go back. Yes, you
must go back!"

And then he stole swiftly away among the
rushes, and Harry heard him talking in
the same low voice to them.

Presently there was a slight noise again
behind them, and on looking round they
beheld the little Child-shadow, with the
beautiful face and wistful eyes. He held in
his hands a faded wreath of cowslips and
daisies and a branch of white May, and on
one of the dried flowers there sat a dead
butterfly, with snow-white wings, looking as
though it were still alive and could fly again
over the sweet green fields, as it was wont to
do in those long-past summer hours. "These
were my playthings," said he; "but only a few
of them: I used to find them long ago in the
meadows, which were full of flowers and
beautiful things, and now the hawthorn tree
has come to live here, for they cut it down
to make a railway, and I went to it only an
hour ago and it gave me this branch as
a keepsake, and it is weary already with
being in Shadow-land. I used to be happy

and play all day long in the lane where it used to grow. If I could only go back there again, and if it could only be all just as it was before!"

"Ah!" said the Boots, "that is not the big world's way. It is full of cruel changes, and is always sending people and things away to live in Shadow-land. But it is always trying to follow them and see them again,—yes, more, even more than you all here long to see them. For you are on your way home, but they are obliged to think of you, who are unattainable and happy, and harmless and good."

But the Child-shadow alone of all the lovely Shadow-spirits refused to be comforted, and mourned for his lost brother. His thoughts were always with the cowslip-wreaths and the rambles in the golden-hued meadows, and he saw them with that clear eye of childhood's memory which refuses ever to forget. Then the Boots took pity on him, and told him more than he had done before.

"You see those distant hills," said they,

pointing to the furthest range behind all the
others.; "if you look there for two or three
days attentively, you will see a shining
speck in the air. And as it advances you
will see that it is a human being who has
left the busy world, and is on his way home
clothed in a white dress. And when it
comes near you will see your old companion
once more, and he will be more glad to see
you even than you to see him, and you will
together fly far away from Shadow-land, with
a heart younger even and more happy than
the little child's among the meadow-flowers."

And this made the little wistful Shadow-
spirit so happy, that he threw away the dead
flowers and thought of them no more, and
danced joyfully away to welcome his old
playmate, with his eyes fixed steadfastly upon
the horizon bounded by the distant hills.

" The young man is sick of the world,
and its beating life is ebbing fast within
him," said the Boots; " and he thinks
perpetually of the little Child-shadow, and
that is why, no doubt, the little one thus longs
to see him. He will soon be here, and then

there will be one Shadow less and one more happy human being."

Harry and the Boots looked at the re-treating form of the Child-shadow till they could scarcely see him, and in a few more moments their vision was obscured by three graceful figures, which danced towards them over the Lake, chanting together a song so tender, beautiful, and plaintive, that they felt spell-bound, and presently there stood before them the three Fairy-spirits. They waved their magic wands around them, and they sang—

"Ah! wherefore beat with mournful plaint
　The waves upon the lonely shore!
Ah! wherefore echoes back the sound
　From cliff and headland evermore!"

At this Harry said, in a whisper, "But there are *no* waves!"

"Hush!" replied the Boots, "it's a poetical licence."

"What's that?" persisted Harry.

"A—well—a licence to say anything that comes into your head. For instance, if you wanted to speak of a tea-spoon you might call it a sugar-mixer. It would be more poetical."

" Oh ! " said Harry.

" Hush ! " said the Boots. The Fairies went on—

> " Sad voices yet more sweet than sad
>   Within the vault of heaven whirled,
> That count the silent throbs which move
>   The worn face of the patient world.

> " And then in Shadow-land there comes—"

" *Me !* " cried a lusty voice, accompanied by a far-spreading light—a golden light, whose beams spread everywhere. " It 's me ! Hide little Shadows, or I shall find you. I am *wide* awake." And peeping over the placid Lake, there rose and smiled the broad face of the shining Sun !—

CHAPTER XVII.

HOME AT LAST.

—It shone straight across Harry's little white bed, and by that bed stood his Mamma, and on it sat little Lily, with a cowslip ball in her dimpled hand. And she was in the act of saying, "Mamma, he is *wide* awake!"

A light seemed to break on Harry's mind, and he said, "Is tea ready?"

"Tea!" echoed his Mamma. "Tea!" exclaimed Eliza. "Well, Master Harry, I should just think it was! Well, sir, I hope you won't never go near that nasty brook again,—Oh, dear! and it all came of them horrid old *boots!*"

"Where are they?" asked Harry, immediately. "Don't you know they're the best Boots in the world?"

" Where are they ?" cried old Eliza.
" Why the gardener's boy has got them ; and
much good they are to him, old down-at-
heel things ! "

"Fetch them instantly ! " cried Harry.
" Give him my little slippers—a new pair—
anything—only let me have my dear old
Boots again ! "

" Go, nurse," said his Mamma, who was
evidently determined to humour Harry ; and
with a shrug of her shoulders and a muttered
" wonder as to what things would come to
when old boots were to be brought right up
into the clean bed-rooms," Eliza departed.

And when she was gone, Harry asked his
Mamma where he had been all this long
while, for he knew now that it was not the
same day on which he had waded in the
brook in the wood, with Eliza and his little
sister sitting by. And his Mamma told him,
as gently as might be, that "the big, ill-fitting
boots had tripped him up, and he had hurt his
forehead against a stone in the brook ; and
that Robert, who was passing by, had taken
him home, quite sleepy and dripping, and

they had put him to bed. And there he had
slept for hours and hours, till they had wondered if he was ever going to wake again,
till Harry's Papa had sent for the Doctor,
who said there wasn't much the matter with
him, only when he awoke he was to take
some physic—doctors always say that; so
then he *had* awoke and—. Now, dear,"
said his Mamma, "I think you had better
take it !"

Harry thought this a very commonplace
ending to his wonderful journeys, and an-
nounced his intention of getting up soon and
going to see his pony ; but, meanwhile, as he
was in bed, and had nothing particular to
do, he gave his Mamma and little sister an
account of his travels far away in the great
world, and all the strange sights that he had
seen.

While he was thus engaged, Eliza came
in, and in her hand she held the identical
pair Harry had found. The *very* same!

"Ah," said Harry, "I see they are nothing particular, after all, and I'm sure
they can't be my dear old Boots, that

took me everywhere. *They* were *Fairy Boots !"*

Nevertheless, he seemed to like to look at them, probably for association's sake, though they were just like other old boots, and never hopped, nor proposed to go anywhere, nor said a word; and so they were allowed, all dirty and all torn as they were, to remain standing quietly on the hearthrug side by side.

And then Harry had his tea.

THE END.

LONDON : PRINTED BY
EDWARD J. FRANCIS, TOOK'S COURT,
CHANCERY LANE, E.C.

DECEMBER, 1873.

SAMUEL TINSLEY'S

PUBLICATIONS.

LONDON:

SAMUEL TINSLEY, Publisher,

10, SOUTHAMPTON STREET, STRAND, W.C.

‚ *Totally distinct from any other firm of Publishers.*

NOTICE.

The *PRINTING* and *PUBLICATION* of all Classes of *BOOKS, Pamphlets, &c.—* *Apply to* MR. SAMUEL TINSLEY, *Publisher,* 10, *Southampton Street, Strand, London, W.C.*

SAMUEL TINSLEY'S
NEW PUBLICATIONS.

THE POPULAR NEW NOVELS, AT ALL LIBRARIES IN TOWN AND COUNTRY.

KITTY'S RIVAL. By SYDNEY MOSTYN, Author of 'The Surgeon's Secret,' etc. 3 vols., 31s. 6d.

CRUEL CONSTANCY. By KATHARINE KING, Author of 'The Queen of the Regiment.' 3 vols., 31s. 6d.

"Miss Katharine King is among the small number of novelists who do not disdain advice. Her present work is a much better novel than 'Lost for Gold.' . . . . The plot is very original, and the atmosphere of the story is healthy, full of breezy, open-air life, of cheerfulness, and harmless fun."— *Spectator.*

"In this story Miss King has made an advance. She has avoided many of the faults which are so apparent in 'Lost for Gold,' and she has bestowed much pains upon delineation of character and descriptions of Irish life. Her book possesses originality."—*Morning Post.*

"The story is told in a concise and workman-like manner, and some scenes of Indian life are written with considerable spirit."—*Daily News.*

"There are some well-written descriptions of Indian life, though the Irish part of the story is the most successful."—*Athenæum.*

"A well-written and thoroughly attractive story."—*Sunday Times.*

TOO LIGHTLY BROKEN. 3 vols. 31s. 6d.

"A very pleasing story . . . . . very prettily told."—*Morning Post.*

THE HEIR OF REDDESMONT. 3 vols., 31s. 6d.

TOWER HALLOWDEANE. 2 vols., 21s.

ANNALS of the TWENTY-NINTH CENTURY; or, the Autobiography of the Tenth President of the World-Republic. 3 vols., 31s. 6d.

Samuel Tinsley, 10, Southampton Street, Strand.

THE MAGIC OF LOVE. By Mrs. Forrest-Grant, Author of ' Fair, but not Wise.' 3 vols., 31s. 6d.

TWIXT CUP and LIP. By Mary Lovett-Cameron. 3 vols., 31s. 6d.

IS IT FOR EVER ? By Kate Mainwaring. 3 vols., 31s. 6d.

"A work to be recommended. . . . . A thrillingly sensational novel."—*Sunday Times*.

FOLLATON PRIORY. 2 vols., 21s.

" 'Follaton Priory' is a thoroughly sensational story, written with more art than is usual in compositions of its class ; and avoiding, skilfully, a melancholy termination."— *Sunday Times*.

ALDEN OF ALDENHOLME. By George Smith. 3 vols., 31s. 6d.

" Pure and graceful. . . . . Above the average."—*Athenæum*.

AS THE FATES WOULD HAVE IT. By G. Beresford Fitzgerald. Crown 8vo., 10s. 6d.

THE BARONET'S CROSS. By Mary Meeke, Author of " Marion's Path through Shadow to Sunshine." 2 vols., 21s.

"A novel suited to the palates of eager consumers of fiction."—*Sunday Times*.

BETWEEN TWO LOVES. By Robert J. Griffiths, LL.D. 3 vols., 31s. 6d.

BUILDING UPON SAND. By Elizabeth J. Lysaght. Crown 8vo., 10s. 6d.

" It is an eminently lady-like story, and pleasantly told. . . . . We can safely recommend 'Building upon Sand.' "—*Graphic*.

THE D'EYNCOURTS OF FAIRLEIGH. By Thomas Rowland Skemp. 3 vols., 31s. 6d.

"An exceedingly readable novel, full of various and sustained interest. . . . . The interest is well kept up all through."—*Daily Telegraph*.

A DESPERATE CHARACTER: a Tale of the Gold Fever. By W. Thomson-Gregg. 3 vols., 31s. 6d.

" A novel which cannot fail to interest."—*Daily News*.

FIRST AND LAST. By F. Vernon-White. 2 vols., 21s.

FAIR, BUT NOT WISE. By Mrs. FORREST-GRANT.
2 vols., 21s.

" 'Fair but not Wise' possesses considerable merit, and is both cleverly
and powerfully written. If earnest, it is yet amusing and sometimes
humorous, and the interest is well sustained from the first to the last
page."—*Court Express.*

GOLDEN MEMOIRS. By EFFIE LEIGH. 2 vols.,
21s.

"There is not a dull page in the book."—*Morning Post.*

GRAYWORTH: a Story of Country Life. By CAREY
HAZELWOOD. 3 vols., 21s. 6d.

"Carey Hazelwood can write well."—*Examiner.*
"Many traces of good feeling and good taste, little touches of quiet
humour, denoting kindly observation, and a genuine love of the country."—
Standard.

HILLESDEN ON THE MOORS. By ROSA MAC-
KENZIE KETTLE, Author of "The Mistress of Langdale
Hall." 2 vols., 21s.

"Thoroughly enjoyable, full of pleasant thoughts gracefully expressed,
and eminently pure in tone."—*Public Opinion.*

NEARER AND DEARER. By ELIZABETH J.
LYSAGHT, Author of "Building upon Sand." 3 vols.,
31s. 6d.

"A capital story. . . very pleasant reading . . . With the expec-
tion of George Eliot, there is no other of our lady writers with whom Mrs.
Lysaght will not favourably compare."—*Scotsman.*
"We have said the book is readable. It is more, it is both clever and
interesting."—*Sunday Times.*

NO FATHERLAND. By MADAME VON OPPEN.
2 vols., 21s.

NOT TO BE BROKEN. By W. A. CHANDLER.
Crown 8vo., 10s. 6d.

PERCY LOCKHART. By F. W. BAXTER. 2 vols.,
21s.

"A bright, fresh, healthy story. . . . . Eminently readable."—
Standard.
"The novel altogether deserves praise. It is healthy in tone, interesting
in plot and incident, and generally so well written that few persons would
be able justly to find fault with it."—*Scotsman.*

Samuel Tinsley, 10, Southampton Street, Strand.

SONS OF DIVES. 2 vols., 21s.

"A well-principled and natural story."—*Athenæum*.

STRANDED, BUT NOT LOST. By Dorothy Bromyard. 3 vols., 31s. 6d.

THE SECRET OF TWO HOUSES. By Fanny, Fisher. 2 vols., 21s.

"Thoroughly dramatic."—*Public Opinion*.
"The story is well told."—*Sunday Times*.

THE SEDGEBOROUGH WORLD. By A. Farebrother. 2 vols., 21s.

"There is no little novelty and a large fund of amusement in 'The Sedgeborough World.'"—*Illustrated London News*.

TIMOTHY CRIPPLE; or, "Life's a Feast." By Thomas Auriol Robinson. 2 vols., 21s.

"This is a most amusing book, and the author deserves great credit for the novelty of his design, and the quaint humour with which it is worked out."—*Public Opinion*.
"For abundance of humour, variety of incident, and idiomatic vigour of expression, Mr. Robinson deserves, and will no doubt receive, great credit."—*Civil Service Review*.

THE TRUE STORY OF HUGH NOBLE'S FLIGHT. By the Authoress of "What Her Face Said." 10s. 6d.

"A pleasant story, with touches of exquisite pathos, well told by one who is master of an excellent and sprightly style."—*Standard*.
"An unpretending, yet very pathetic story. . . . We can congratulate the author on having achieved a signal success."—*Graphic*.

THE INSIDIOUS THIEF: a Tale for Humble Folks. By One of Themselves. Crown 8vo., 5s. Second Edition.

WAGES: a Story in Three Books. 3 vols., 31s. 6d.

"A work of no commonplace character."—*Sunday Times*.

WEIMAR'S TRUST. By Mrs. Edward Christian. 3 vols., 31s. 6d.

"A novel which deserves to be read, and which, once begun, will not be readily laid aside till the end."—*Scotsman*.

THE SURGEON'S SECRET. By SYDNEY MOSTYN,
Author of "Kitty's Rival," etc. Crown 8vo., 10s. 6d.

"A most exciting novel—the best on our list. It may be fairly recommended as a very extraordinary book."—*John Bull.*

"A stirring drama, with a number of closely-connected scenes, in which there are not a few legitimately sensational situations. There are many spirited passages."—*Public Opinion.*

"This is a good novel. . . The descriptions of country life are so spirited that the book may be read from beginning to end with unflagging interest. . . . The character of the heroine is also attractive and winning. The work is, undoubtedly, one to be sought for at the libraries."—*Sunday Times.*

"Shows very considerable marks of the ability of the author. The writing of the story is very brisk. The story will be read with interest by that very numerous class who devour all such books with great eagerness, if they but contain something of mystery and a good deal of interest. Both these are found in Mr. Mostyn's book, and therefore it should be a favourite with the class to whom allusion has been made."—*Scotsman.*

WILL SHE BEAR IT? A Tale of the Weald.
3 vols., 31s. 6d.

"This is a clever story, easily and naturally told, and the reader's interest sustained throughout. . . . A pleasant, readable book, such as we can heartily recommend as likely to do good service in the dull and foggy days before us."—*Spectator.*

"Written with simplicity, good feeling, and good sense, and marked throughout by a high moral tone, which is all the more powerful from never being obtrusive. . . . The interest is kept up with increasing power to the last."—*Standard.*

"The story is a love tale, and the interest is almost entirely confined to the heroine, who is certainly a good girl, bearing unmerited sorrow with patience and resignation. The heroine's young friend is also attractive. . . . As for the seventh commandment, its breach is not even alluded to."—*Athenæum.*

"There is abundance of individuality in the story, the characters are all genuine, and the atmosphere of the novel is agreeable. It is really interesting. On the whole, it may be recommended for general perusal."—*Sunday Times.*

"'Will She Bear it?' is a story of English country life. . . . It is no small praise to say that the tone of the book throughout is thoroughly pure and healthy, without being either dull or namby-pamby."—*Illustrated Review.*

"A story of English country life in the early part of this century, thoroughly clever and interesting, and pleasantly and naturally told. . . . . In every way we entertain a very high opinion of this book."—*Graphic.*

TOM DELANY. By ROBERT THYNNE, Author of "Ravensdale." 3 vols., 31s. 6d.

"Town life and station life, the life of the diggings, and the life of the road are set most vividly before us. We parch on Australian plains ; we freeze on Alpine summits ; we are cheered in our depths of despondency by Captain Kinnegad, and assisted in our rejoicing over happier circumstances by the joyous companionship of the enterprising Mr. Bayley. . . . Irishmen and Australians will appreciate this book."—*Athenæum*.

"Mr. Bayley, as he is always called, is one of the best characters in the book, and the love-making between him and Loo is often amusing. But, perhaps, the most important member is one, Captain Kinnegad, 'a middle-aged gentleman of battered appearance.' No one knew—in all probability he did not himself know—in what service exactly it was he had gained h rank of captain. . . . The description of Australia in most respects seems so life-like that we find it hard to believe that Mr. Thynne writes what he has never seen."—*Saturday Review*.

"The chapters descriptive of the progress of Mr. Brigg's ailment are all forcible. It may be doubted whether anywhere in fiction there is a more stiking account of what are so appropriately called the 'horrors'—De Foe has little that is more graphic and distinct. . . . We heartily commend 'Tom Delany' as a novel from which the reader is certain to derive great amusement, and from which it is possible he might obtain instruction also."—*Sunday Times*.

"Here and there will be found passages of great power, such as the chapter, for example, in which one of the heroines escapes from one of the deadliest of Australian snakes. . . . This is a very bright, healthy, simply-told story."—*Standard*.

"All the individuals whom the reader meets at the gold-fields are well-drawn, amongst whom not the least interesting is 'Terrible Mac.'"—*Hour*.

"Although there are numerous characters introduced, they are all so fully described, and distinct from one another, that they remain stedfastly before the reader's eye without any effort of memory on his part."—*Irish Daily Telegraph*.

"There is not a dull page in the book."—*Scotsman*.

BY THE SAME AUTHOR.

RAVENSDALE. By ROBERT THYNNE, Author of "Tom Delany." 3 vols., 31s. 6d.

"A well-told, natural, and wholesome story."—*Standard*.

"No one can deny merit to the writer."—*Saturday Review*.

"The interest of a well managed and very complicated plot is sustained to the end ; and the fresh, healthy tone of the book, as well as the command of language possessed by its author in such a remarkable degree, will insure for it a wide popularity, as it contrasts strongly with the vapid and sentimental, as well as with the sensational publications so rife at the present day."—*Morning Post*.

Notice:

NEW SYSTEM OF PUBLISHING ORIGINAL NOVELS.

VOL. I.

THE MISTRESS OF LANGDALE HALL: a Romance of the West Riding. By ROSA MACKENZIE KETTLE. Complete in one handsome volume, with Frontispiece and Vignette by PERCIVAL SKELTON. 4s., post free.

(*From THE SATURDAY REVIEW.*)

Generally speaking, in criticising a novel we confine our observations to the merits of the author. In this case we must make an exception, and say something as to the publisher. The *Mistress of Langdale Hall* does not come before us in the stereotyped three-volume shape, with rambling type, ample margins, and nominally a guinea and a half to pay. On the contrary, this new aspirant to public admiration appears in the modest guise of a single graceful volume, and we confess that we are disposed to give a kindly welcome to the author, because we may flatter ourselves that she is in some measure a *protégée* of our own. A few weeks ago an article appeared in our columns censuring the prevailing fashion of publishing novels at nominal and fancy prices. Necessarily, we dealt a good deal in commonplaces, the absurdity of the fashion being so obvious. We explained, what is well known to every one interested in the matter, that the regulation price is purely illusory. The publisher in reality has to drive his own bargain with the libraries, who naturally beat him down. The author suffers, the trade suffers, and the libraries do not gain. Arguing that a palpable absurdity must be exploded some day unless all the world is qualified for Bedlam, we felt ourselves on tolerably safe ground when we ventured to predict an approaching revolution. Judging from the preface to this book, we may conjecture that it was partly on our hint that Mr. Tinsley has published. As all prophets must welcome events that tend to the speedy accomplishment of their predictions, we confess ourselves gratified by the promptitude with which Mr. Tinsley has acted, and we heartily wish his venture success. He recognises that a reformation so radical must be a work of time, and at first may possibly seem to defeat its object. For it is plain that the public must first be converted to a proper regard for its own interest ; and, by changing the borrowing for the buying system, must come in to buy the publisher out. He must look, moreover, to the support and imitation of his brethren of the trade. We doubt not he has made the venture after all due deliberation, and that we may rely on his determination seconding his enterprise. All prospectuses of new undertakings tend naturally to exaggeration, but success will be well worth the waiting for, should it be only the shadow of that on which Mr. Tinsley reckons. He gives some surprising figures ; he states some startling facts ; and, as a practical man, he draws some practical conclusions. He quotes a state-ment of Mr. Charles Reade's, to the effect that three publishers in the United States had disposed of no less than 370,000 copies of Mr. Reade's latest novel. He estimates that the profits on that sale—the book being published at a dollar—must amount to £25,000. Mr. Reade, of course, has a name, and we can conceive that his faults and blemishes may positively recommend themselves to American taste. But Mr. Tinsley remarks that if a publisher could sell 70,000 copies in any case, there would still be £5,000 of clear gain ; and even if the new system had a much more moderate success than that, all parties would still profit amazingly. For Mr. Tinsley calculates the profits of a sale of 2,000 copies of a three volume edition at £1,000; and we should fancy the experience of most authors would lead them to believe he overstates it. It will be seen that at all events the new speculation promises bril-liantly, and reason and common-sense conspire to tell us that the reward must come to him who has patience to wait. *Palmam qui meruit ferat*, and may he have his share of the profits too. Meanwhile, here we have the first volume of Mr. Tinsley's new series in most legible type, in portable form, and with a sufficiently attractive exterior. The price is four shillings, and, the customary trade deduction being made to circulating libraries, it leaves them without excuse should they deny it to the order of their customers.

We should apologise to Miss Kettle for keeping her waiting while we discuss business matters with her publisher. But she knows, no doubt, that there are times when business must take precedence of pleasure, and conscientious readers are bound to dispose of the preface before proceeding to the book. For we may say at once that ·we have found pleasure in reading her story. In the first place, it has a strong and natural local colouring, and we always like anything that gives a book individuality. In the next, there is a feminine grace about her pictures of nature and delineations of female character, and that always makes a story attractive. Finally, there is a certain interest that carries us along, although the story is loosely put together, and the demands on our credulity are somewhat incessant and importunate. The scene is laid in the West Riding of Yorkshire ; nor did it need the dedication of the book to tell us that the author was an old resident in the county. With considerable artistic subtlety she lays her scenes in the very confines of busy life. Cockneys and professional foreign tourists are much in the way of believing that the manufacturing districts are severed from the genuinely rural ones by a hard-

and-fast line ; that the demons of cotton, coal, and wool blight everything within the scope of their baleful influence. There can be no greater blunder ; native intelligence might tell us that mills naturally follow water power, and that a broad stream and a good fall generally imply wooded banks and sequestered ravines, swirling pools, and rushing rapids. Miss Kettle, as a dweller in the populous and flourishing West Riding, has learned all that, of course. She is aware besides of the power of contrast ; that peace and solitude are never so much appreciated as when you have just quitted the bustle of life, and hear its hum mellowed by the distance. Romance is never so romantic as when it rubs shoulders with the practical, and sensation 'piles itself up' when it is evolved in the centre of common-place life. . . . . . .

The story is interesting and very pleasantly written, and for the sake of both author and publisher we cordially wish it the reception it deserves.

"The most careful mother need not hesitate to place it at once in the hands of the most unsophisticated daughter. As regards the publisher, we can honestly say that the type is clear and the book well got up in every way."—*Athenæum.*

"There is a naturalness in this novel, published in accordance with Mr. Tinsley's very wholesome one-volumed system."—*Spectator.*

"'The Mistress of Langdale Hall' is a bright and attractive story, which can be read from beginning to end with pleasure."—*Daily News.*

"A charming 'Romance of the West Riding,' full of grace and pleasing incident."—*Public Opinion.*

"The story is really well told, and some of the characters are delineated with great vividness and force. The tone of the book is high." —*Non-conformist.*

"It is a good story, with abundant interest, and a purity of thought and language which is much rarer in novels than it ought to be. The volume is handsomely got up, and contains a well-drawn vignette and frontispiece."—*Scotsman.*

"Not only is it written with good taste and good feeling,—it is never dull, while at the same time it is quite devoid of sensationalism or extravagance It deals with life in the West Riding."—*Globe.*

"The book is admirably got up, and contains an introductory circular by the publisher."—*Civil Service Gazette.*

"A model of what a cheap novel should be."—*Publisher's Circular.*

Samuel Tinsley, 10, Southampton Street, Strand.

"A circular from the publisher precedes the opening of the novel, wherein the existing conditions of novel-publishing are concisely set forth. It is ably and smartly written, and forms by no means the least interesting portion of the contents of the volume. We strongly recommend its perusal to novel readers generally."—*Welshman*.

"Few will take up this entertaining volume without feeling compelled to go through with it. We cannot entertain a doubt as to the success of this novel, and the remarks made by the publisher in his prefatory circular are of the most sensible and practical kind."—*Hull Packet*.

"For this district the '*Mistress of Langdale Hall*' has a peculiar interest."—*Leeds Mercury*.

Vol. II.

PUTTYPUT'S PROTÉGÉE; or, Road, Rail, and River. A Story in Three Books. By HENRY GEORGE CHURCHILL. Crown 8vo., (uniform with "The Mistress of Langdale Hall"), with 14 illustrations by WALLIS MACKAY. Post free, 4s. Second edition.

"It is a lengthened and diversified farce, full of screaming fun and comic delineation—a reflection of Dickens, Mrs. Malaprop, and Mr. Boucicault, and dealing with various descriptions of social life. We have read and laughed, pooh-poohed, and read again, ashamed of our interest, but our interest has been too strong for our shame. Readers may do worse than surrender themselves to its melo-dramatic enjoyment. From title-page to colophon, only Dominie Sampson's epithet can describe it—it is 'prodigious.'"—*British Quarterly Review*.

"It is impossible to read 'Puttyput's Protégée' without being reminded at every turn of the contemporary stage, and the impression it leaves on the mind is very similar to that produced by witnessing a whole evening's entertainment at one of our popular theatres."—*Echo*.

Samuel Tinsley, 10, Southampton Street, Strand.

FLORENCE; or, Loyal Quand Même. By FRANCES ARMSTRONG. Crown 8vo., 5s., cloth. Post free.

"It is impossible not be interested in the story from beginning to end. . . . We congratulate Mr. Samuel Tinsley on continuing to break at intervals the monotonous line of three-volume novels."—*Examiner*.

"A very charming love story, eminently pure and lady-like in tone, effective and interesting in plot, and, rarest praise of all, written in excellent English."—*Civil Service Review*.

"We should gladly welcome many more such novels, in preference to the trash which but too frequently passes current for such."—*Brighton Observer*.

"We cannot close this very interesting work without commending it to every reader."—*Durham County Advertiser*.

"The book is excellently printed and nicely bound—in fact it is one which authoress, publisher, and reader may alike regard with mingled satisfaction and pleasure."—*Nottingham Daily Guardian*.

"'Florence' is readable, even interesting in every part."—*The Scotsman*.

"Suffice it to say that from beginning to end each character is well brought out, and what is perhaps best of all, there is a healthy vigour and genuine ring about the whole composition which goes far to show that a truly chaste tone, sustained throughout, is in no way incompatible with a most engrossing story."—*Cornish Telegraph*.

"'Florence' is a healthy, high-toned story, which every one can read with pleasure and gratification. . . . The author writes with vivacity and effect. To her the creation of Florence has evidently been a labour of love, and we feel convinced that few readers will close the book without feeling that they share in the affection with which the heroine is regarded b the author."—*Leeds Mercury*.

"Several of the characters introduced are drawn with a master hand, Florence herself being especially worthy of admiration."—*Hastings and St. Leonards Advertiser*.

"The book is decidedly far superior in tone to the generality of novels, and is well worth reading. . . . Miss Armstrong gives us much ground for hope that her pen will be fertile."—*Lloyd's Weekly Newspaper*.

"'Florence' is therefore (as we said to begin with) a pleasant and readable story, and as its influences cannot be otherwise than beneficial, we hope it will be widely read."—*Edinburgh Daily Review*.

"It is essentially a lady's book, and is deserving of the highest praise."—*Irish Daily Telegraph*.

"We cordially wish the work may meet with the success it deserves; but of this we have no doubt."—*Derbyshire Courier*.

"Miss Armstrong has written a very agreeable story, much more interesting than many three-volume novels it has been our misfortune to read. . . . Instead of spinning out a dreary, colourless romance of interminable length, Miss Armstrong has preferred to present to her readers a bright, lively, natural story of every day life."—*Public Opinion*.

Samuel Tinsley, 10, Southampton Street, Strand.

EPITAPHIANA; or, the Curiosities of Churchyard Literature : being a Miscellaneous Collection of Epitaphs, with an INTRODUCTION. By W. FAIRLEY. Crown 8vo., cloth, price 5s. Post free.

"An amusing book. . . . A capital collection of epitaphs."—*Court Circular.*

"Mr. Fairley's industry has been rewarded by an assemblage of grotesque and fantastic epitaphs, such as we never remember to have seen equalled. They fill an elegantly printed volume."—*Cork Examiner.*

"Although we have picked several plums from Mr. Fairley's book, we can assure our readers that there are plenty more left. And now that the long evenings are once more stealing upon us, and the fireside begins to be comfortable, suggesting a book and a quiet read, let us recommend Mr. Fairley, who comes before us in the handsome guise and the capital type of the enterprising Mr. Samuel Tinsley."—*Derbyshire Advertiser.*

"His collection is not only amusing, but has a certain historical value, as illustrating the rough humour in which our forefathers frequently indulged at the expense of the departed."—*Staffordshire Advertiser.*

"We have quoted enough to show that Mr. Fairley has produced a curious and entertaining volume, which will well repay perusal."—*Oxford Chronicle.*

"On the score of novelty, at least, 'Epitaphiana' will attract considerable attention."—*Irish Daily Telegraph.*

"Mr. Fairley has a keen eye for a quaint epitaph, and an excellent sense of what is humorous or pathetic. . . . The volume contains an excellent introduction relating to ancient and modern burials, and is published in an attractive form."—*Civil Service Gazette.*

"Mr. Fairley has made a quaint and curious collection."—*The Court Circular.*

"A very interesting book, the materials industriously gathered from many cities of the Silent Land, and the miscellaneous collection carefully prepared for publication."—*Colliery Guardian.*

"In noticing this most interesting book, we feel we can commend it in all sincerity ; for just as a chapter from 'Pickwick' is an antidote to *ennui,* 'Epitaphiana' may be pronounced as equally reviving to dull spirits. . . . The volume itself is quite a work of art."—*The Forester.*

"Mr. Fairley seems to have gathered these scraps from village churchyards and elsewhere, simply for his own amusement, but they have swollen to such proportions that he has been induced to publish them ; and the subject matter of his volume is particularly entertaining."—*Public Opinion.*

"A very readable volume."—*Daily Review.*

SUMMER SHADE AND WINTER SUNSHINE:
Poems. By ROSA MACKENZIE KETTLE, Author of "The
Mistress of Langdale Hall." New Edition. 2s. 6d., cloth.

"Graceful and pleasing."—*Civil Service Review.*

"Contains much charming poetry."—*Civil Service Gazette.*

"Serious in spirit, but cheerful in tone ; hopeful and animated."—*Public Opinion.*

"Marked by great beauty of thought and language."—*Leeds Mercury.*

MARY DESMOND, AND OTHER POEMS. By
NICHOLAS J. GANNON. Fcp. 8vo., 4s., cloth.

"A poem of considerable power."—*Examiner.*

"The story is told in a touching pathetic manner, in words which must touch the most insensible heart."—*Irish Times.*

"Almost all Mr. Gannon's poems are marked by national characteristics and patriotic sentiments."—*Public Opinion.*

"Mr. Gannon's exquisite poetry."—*Dublin Evening Mail.*

"Handles subjects with a creditable skill and happiness."—*Illustrated Review.*

THE WITCH of NEMI, and other Poems. By
EDWARD BRENNAN. Crown 8vo., 10s. 6d.

BALAK AND BALAAM IN EUROPEAN COS-
TUME. By the Rev. JAMES KEAN, M.A., Assistant to
the Incumbent of Markinch, Fife. 6d., sewed.

ANOTHER ROW AT DAME EUROPA'S SCHOOL.
Showing how John's Cook made an IRISH STEW, and
what came of it. 6d., sewed.

THE GOLDEN PATH: a Poem. By ISABELLA
STUART. 6d., sewed.

THE FALL OF MAN: An Answer to Mr. Darwin's
"Descent of Man ;" being a Complete Refutation, by
common-sense arguments, of the Theory of Natural Selection.
1s., sewed.

THE REDBREAST OF CANTERBURY CATHE-
DRAL : Lines from the Latin of Peter du Moulin, sometime a Prebendary of Canterbury. Translated by the Rev.
F. B. WELLS, M.A., Rector of Woodchurch. Handsomely
bound, price 1s.

Samuel Tinsley, 10, Southampton Street, Strand.

HARRY'S BIG BOOTS : a Fairy Tale, for "Smalle
Folke." By S. E. GAY. With 8 Full-page Illustrations
and a Vignette by the author, drawn on wood by PERCIVAL
SKELTON. Crown 8vo., handsomely bound in cloth, price 5s.

From the *Daily News*, Nov. 24th, 1873 :—"'Harry's Big Boots' is sure
of a large and appreciative audience. It is as good as a Christmas panto-
mime, and its illustrations are, quite equal to any transformation scene.
Perhaps the somewhat heavy satire on Primitive Prim, a little man who is
'evolved' out of a periwinkle and who hardens into a fossil, may be lost on
the little people. But the fun about deep-sea dredging and the 'fashionable
waggonette,' which the sea-people make out of the scientific gentleman's
dredger, will no doubt amply compensate for anything the young readers
do not quite understand; while the pictures of Harry and Harry's seven-
leagued boots, with their little wings and funny faces, leave nothing to be
desired."

THE PHYSIOLOGY OF THE SECTS. Crown
8vo., price 5s.

ANOTHER WORLD; or, Fragments from the Star
City of Montalluyah. By HERMES. Third Edition, re-
vised, with additions. Post 8vo., price 12s.

"A very curious book, very clearly written. . . . . Likely to contain hints on a vast number of subjects of interest to mankind."—*Saturday Review*.
"Hermes is a really practical philosopher, and utters many truths that
must be as useful to this sublunary sphere as to those of another world.
. . . . Of his powers of narrative and expression there can be no
doubt."—*Morning Post*.
"A romance of science. . . . Few volumes that have ever come
under our hands are more entertaining to read or more difficult to criticise."
—*Sunday Times*.
"We can recommend 'Another World' as decidedly clever and
original."—*Literary World*.
"Whether one reads for information or for amusement, 'Another World'
will attract and retain the attention. It reminds one somewhat of Swift's
'Gulliver,' without the grossness and the ill-nature."—*Standard*.
"'Another World' can be safely recommended as sure to afford amuse-
ment, combined with no little instruction."—*Echo*.

www.ingramcontent.com/pod-product-compliance
Lightning Source LLC
Chambersburg PA
CBHW030819020726
47499CB00006B/1979